A DOG DETECTIVE SHORT STORY COLLECTION

A DOG DETECTIVE SHORT STORY COLLECTION

SANDRA BAUBLITZ

No part of this publication may be reproduced, stored in a retrieval system, or transmitted, in any form or by any means, without the prior permission in writing of the publisher, nor be otherwise circulated in any form of binding or cover other than that in which it is published and without a similar condition including this condition being imposed on the subsequent purchaser.

FBI Anti-Piracy Warning: The unauthorized reproduction or distribution of a copyrighted work is illegal. Criminal copyright infringement, including infringement without monetary gain, is investigated by the FBI and is punishable by up to five years in federal prison and a fine of $250,000.

This is a work of fiction. Names, places, businesses, and people are the imagination of the author and fictitious. Any resemblance to actual people (living or dead), places, or names/businesses is purely coincidental.

All rights reserved. Your support of the author's rights is appreciated.

A DOG DETECTIVE SHORT STORY COLLECTION

ISBN: 978-1544036717

Copyright © 2017 Sandra Baublitz

Author website: www.sandrabaublitz.com

Cover art by SwoonWorthy Book Covers

www.bookcover-designs.blogspot.com

V3

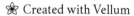 Created with Vellum

The author wishes to thank:
Lisa Shea, for her mentoring, editing, and friendship.
Sherry Soule, for her outstanding book covers.
Her mother, Goldie Baublitz, for her encouragement and support.
And Clarissa and Paw's fans whose support keeps these stories alive.

1

THE MYSTERY OF THE BLUE DOLPHINS

1990s

The bright sunshine highlighting the orange and red of the fall leaves seemed to lessen my melancholy mood. I was driving through upstate New York to visit my cousin, Lucinda. My name is Clarissa Montgomery Hayes, freelance writer, mystery lover, and dog owner. The dog in question is Paudius Pernivius - Paw, for short, due to his love of digging in the wrong places at the worst times.

Anyway, Paw and I were on our way to cheer up Cousin Lucinda after the recent death of our uncle, Josh. Lucinda's parents had been killed in a tragic car crash when she was ten years old. Josh and his wife, Mavis, had taken Lucinda into their home and raised her.

Lucinda liked her aunt, but she adored her uncle, and

they were devoted to each other. His sudden death two months ago from a heart attack had hit her quite hard.

I hadn't seen the family for many years. We had grown apart after Lucinda moved in with Josh and Mavis.

I pulled in front of the old Victorian home where until recently the trio lived in harmony. Lucinda came out to greet me. She was dressed in a yellow plaid jumper with a beautifully engraved silver clover locket. She was smiling, but her eyes betrayed her sadness.

Lucinda, thirty, was always the beautiful one with auburn hair and clear blue eyes. She had the grace of a swan.

In my mid-twenties, with blonde hair and hazel eyes, I was no match for Lucinda's beauty.

Paw jumped out of the car, licked Luce's face, and headed to investigate the garden for chipmunks and other such "enemies."

"How are you?" I asked Lucinda as we embraced.

"Fine," she said and quickly changed the subject. "You're looking well. How was your trip?"

"Everything went well. It was a smooth and easy drive."

"Paw is adorable. I see he has already found the garden."

I turned to see Paw trotting up the path to the garden. "I better get him. Paw loves to dig and I wouldn't want to upset Aunt Mavis. I know she prizes her garden."

As we entered the garden, I saw the furry brown tail of my very large Saint Bernard waving in the air as he dug furiously in a bed of mums.

"Paw, get out of there!" I yelled as I ran toward him. He

gave me one of his "I am innocent" looks and backed away. He had dug up a rather well-used meat bone, but what caught my eye was a corner of shiny plastic. It turned out to be a plastic garbage bag with a red dress inside.

"This is an odd thing to bury in the garden."

"Yes, I've no idea who put it there. I'll take it in the house; perhaps Aunt Mavis will know." Lucinda took the dress and headed for the house.

Entering the house, I was transported back in time. Aunt Mavis and Uncle Josh were avid antiques collectors; this was evident in every room in the house. Uncle Josh had always loved antiques and had had a thorough knowledge of pre-1920s culture.

Aunt Mavis greeted us in the living room. She was a tall, agile woman in her mid-fifties with graying hair and dark brown eyes. I never liked her very much. The set of her chin and the hardness of her eyes always gave me the feeling that she looked down on her niece and friends. I am usually a good judge of character, but the few times I had met Mavis, she had been kind and caring.

Lucinda held up the dress. "Aunt, have you ever seen this dress before?"

"Why it's nearly brand new. No, I've never seen it before. That was so sweet of you to bring Lucinda a gift, Clarissa." Mavis smiled.

I frowned. "I didn't, Aunt Mavis. I have a confession to make. Paw dug it up out of your garden. He dug up some of your lovely mums too."

She scowled at this.

I hurried on, "Don't worry. I will replant the mums and replace any damaged ones."

Aunt Mavis looked displeased, especially when she looked down at Paw who had just stepped into the house. He had dirty paws from digging in the garden.

I blushed. "Sorry. I will take Paw back outside and wash him off. Lucinda, do you have a hose I could use?"

Lucinda began to nod, but Mavis interrupted.

"Don't be silly. Take Paw to the laundry room and wash him. And don't worry about the mums. I will replant them. I love to get out and work in the garden."

I took Paw to the laundry room and began washing him. Of course, I got as wet as he did. Lucinda came in with towels and laughed at us. Just then Paw shook himself and sprayed everything and both of us with water. It took a while but we got him dry, and the room cleaned up.

Lucinda showed me up to my room; overrun with antiques (which I'm not fond of) but with a down comforter on the bed and a window seat (the redeeming qualities), the room had a lived in, homey atmosphere. After getting settled, I had dinner with the family which consisted of Lucinda, Aunt Mavis, Gladys, a neighbor, and Father Henry, the local clergyman. Gossiping Gladys conversed with everyone and knew who was doing what. She was nosy and outspoken where Mavis was refined and demure. However, they had been close friends for years.

Then there was Father Henry. He was forty, a young man by church standards. Either Aunt Mavis or Gladys always invited him to dinner. Since both were high in the church committees, it was deemed necessary to invite Father Henry to everything. And last but not least, there was Nellie Gatewell, the live-in housekeeper.

She was in her late sixties—kind, gentle, and above all loyal.

Following dinner, I went straight to bed. It had been a long day, but I was too restless to sleep. So I sat up and read a while. There was no need for a light because the moon was full.

Suddenly I heard a scraping noise and looked over in time to see something pushed under my door. With lightning speed, Paw was upon the "something" in question. I went over and looked out the door; no one was in sight.

Paw sadly relinquished his treasure — a single a piece of folded notepaper. I opened it and was shocked at the message.

"UNCLE JOSH WAS MURDERED."

The rest of the night was spent in restless sleep as I tried to figure out what it meant and who could have sent the note. It had to be someone in the house, but any of the dinner guests could have slipped the note under my door as I had retired early.

By the morning as I woke with the sunshine on my face, I was nowhere closer to an answer.

At breakfast, as I ate my toast and eggs, I contemplated the note I had tucked in my pocket. My conscience urged me to tell Lucinda about the note's message. But I didn't want to upset Luce. I wanted to find out the truth about my uncle's death before burdening her with the news.

"Luce, I didn't know Uncle Josh was in poor health."

The pain on her face told me she didn't want to talk about it, but she relented and said:

"He wasn't as far as we knew. It was all quite sudden."

"Had he been doing anything particular the day he died? What was he doing? I mean was he overworking himself?"

"No. Uncle Josh spent most of the day in the library. Also, that was the day he bought the new collar for Paw that he sent you, now that I think about it."

I remembered the collar quite well. In fact, Paw was still wearing it. It was the only collar he'd never been able to strip off. The day it arrived I put it on Paw, and he loved the collar. It was a dark blue nylon with an attached nylon bag holding a sandstone; the manufacturer guaranteed it would last. Somehow Paw knew the collar was from Josh; I could see it in his eyes.

Lucinda finished her tea then stood abruptly, shoving in her chair. Her knuckles were white where she gripped the back of the chair. "I'm sorry, but I have to get to the church early. Bingo was last night, and they always use my daycare space for their refreshments. I have to clean up before the kids arrive."

I chastised myself. It was apparent that I had distressed Luce with my questions. I reached across the table and gave one of her hands a squeeze.

She smiled tightly then exited the room.

Aunt Mavis hadn't joined us for breakfast. I picked up my plate and walked to the kitchen to find her.

I entered the kitchen and placed my plate and utensils in

the dishwasher. No one was around. I went upstairs to let Paw out of the guest room and to retrieve my purse.

Paw and I did a quick search of the house and gardens but found no one.

Shrugging, I went outside with Paw. I opened my car door, and Paw jumped into the backseat. I decided to head to the local library to look up Josh's death. A short drive and I was at the library where I nudged Paw to stay in the car.

I went in and was soon searching back copies of the local newspaper. To my surprise, there was very little in the newspapers. The obituary read "death by sudden heart attack". There were no further write-ups. Very strange for a man who had been popular in a small community. However, one name from the obit column caught my attention - Harry Turnapple. He was a pallbearer, but more importantly, he and Josh had been best friends since kindergarten. A quick look in the current phone book gave me an address, and I went in search of Harry.

Harry lived in a small white house on the edge of town. An avid gardener, he had a beautiful bed of begonias and, even at sixty, the energy of a twenty-year-old. As I pulled into the drive, Harry was sitting on his front porch, a golden retriever at his side. I had got out of the car and made it halfway to the porch when Harry gruffly reprimanded me.

"Ya got a dog in that thar car of yourn. Let him out afore he roasts ta death."

Quickly I returned to the car, opening the door for Paw. He was delighted to get out and greet another dog. Now I love Paw and would never want to harm him. I know very well leaving him in the car is wrong, but I wasn't sure how he would react to the golden retriever. Usually, he is good with other dogs, but I didn't want to break up a fight. Upon his release, Paw greeted the golden retriever as only a dog can. They seemed to be fine with each other.

While the dogs got acquainted, I went on the porch to talk to Harry. He smiled watching the dogs sniffing each other, then turned to me.

"Sylvie been needin' some visitors. Don't ya worry none she'n been taken care of. What 'n you wanna see me for? Better not be from the census place!"

"I can assure you that I'm not from the census bureau. I want to talk to you about my uncle, Josh McFarlane."

"Josh, he was a good ole' pal. We were friends afore we's coulda count an' write."

"Yes, I know he valued your friendship. Tell me, Harry, did you know Josh was in bad health?"

"Nah. That man was healthy as a horse. If'n you ask me somebody caught him snoopin' and dun him in."

"Snooping? I don't understand."

"Well, ya see," Harry explained as he settled himself in his chair, "Josh was convinced that all them thar jule theivens were dun by the same fella and he was aimin' to find out who."

"I don't remember hearing about any jewel heists. When did this happen?"

"Aw, good while aready. Ya can go lookin' it up in the

newspapers or if 'n ya wanta ya can go askin' ol' Pete at his'n jule store. He's one of ta fellars that'n got robbed."

"Thank you, Harry. You have been a big help."

"Welcome. Come back and see me and Sylvie soon."

Paw was reluctant to leave Sylvie but eventually climbed into the car. As I started the engine, I realized Pete's jewelry store was on my way home. I might as well stop in.

I parked right out front of the small store.

Paw nudged my shoulder.

"Okay, big guy, you can go in but stay on your best behavior."

He woofed in compliance.

As I entered the store, I kept Paw close to my side. The store had some nice pieces of jewelry, including some rather expensive ones. I stopped by a glass case to admire a pair of ruby earrings. At the sound of footsteps, I turned to see a thin young man approaching me.

He hesitated when he saw Paw. I tensed. Not everyone liked dogs.

The young man grinned and pointed at Paw. "Is he friendly?"

I relaxed. "Yes. He is. You can pet him if you like."

He crouched down to Paw and began to stroke Paw's ears. "Nice dog. My brother has a Saint Bernard. Jasper is incredibly loyal."

I motioned to Paw who was licking the guy's hand. "He is, too."

I extended my hand. "My name is Clarissa Hayes."

The guy stood up and clasped my hand. "Nice to meet you. Name's Carl Sikes. What can I do for you?"

"Do you work here?"

"Sure do. Are you looking for a specific piece of jewelry?"

"No. I'm looking for information about the jewel theft that occurred here a few years ago."

Carl hesitated. "Are you with the police?"

"No. I'm more of an amateur detective."

He laughed. "Really? I'd love to be a private eye. Only I'm stuck here in this dead end job. Don't tell the boss I said that, please?"

Paw woofed. Carl hunched down again. "I know you wouldn't buddy."

He had interpreted Paw's woof as a vow to secrecy when Paw just wanted more caresses.

I cleared my throat. "We won't tell your boss. Do you remember anything about the robbery?"

Carl stood up. "I wasn't here at the time. I've only worked here six months, but I heard some guy got killed. Can you believe it?"

I shook my head in the negative.

He continued, "There had been a string of robberies on and off for several years. I think the theft here happened about two years ago. I never heard what was stolen."

"What happened to the clerk who did work here?"

"You mean Dave? He moved to Michigan."

"Do you think Pete would talk to me?"

A Dog Detective Short Story Collection

"No way. When he heard Dave telling me about the robbery, he fired him."

"Anything else?"

"Nope. Wait, I do remember Dave saying that a woman wearing a red dress was involved."

Hmm, a red dress? Could it be the one Paw found?

I extended my hand again. "Thanks for your help."

We shook, and Carl said, "No problem. If you ever need help on a case, just call me."

I smiled politely and tugged on Paw's collar.

"Let's go, buddy."

As I stepped out of the store with Paw, I was so deep in thought that I collided with someone on the sidewalk.

I looked up into Father Henry's face.

I hadn't noticed it before, but he was a very handsome man. He stood six foot tall, had jet-black hair, and piercing blue eyes. No wonder Aunt Mavis, Gladys, and the rest of the women in town attended church so much.

Paw, on the other hand, gave a low growl. He, obviously, didn't share the same feelings for the clergyman as the women did.

Father Henry and I exchanged pleasantries, and I returned home.

Dinner was enjoyable, but only Lucinda and I were there to eat. We caught up on old times. I told her about visiting Harry, and she showed me pictures of her daycare children. As I left the dining room to go to bed, I passed Aunt Mavis. She seemed to be staring into space but greeted me warmly upon noticing me. Apparently, she thought more highly of me than I did of her.

That night I had the strangest dream. I was walking through town when a wolf started to chase me. I could see its gray and white fur and sharp pointed teeth. Around its neck dangled something shiny. Suddenly, Paw was there to protect me, and the wolf went running into the church.

In the morning, I woke up with the feeling that I should know something. I couldn't remember, though, so I dressed and went to breakfast. After breakfast, I decided to walk to the library. To my delight, of the newspaper articles on the jewel robberies, one held a very concise account. It read as follows:

The Daily Squirer - May 10th

Of the robberies to date by the gang dubbed "The Jewel Fiends," all have followed a similar format. In each case, a very beautiful woman, early twenties, wearing a red dress has entered the store. While she has the store owner distracted her accomplices walk in, tie up the store clerk, and steal the most valuable jewels. As of this date none of the jewels, including a pair of sapphire clip-on earrings known as the Blue Dolphins, have been recovered. However, the last robbery proved tragic. Of the three accomplices, one was shot dead - a man in mid-thirties, tall, well built - identified as Hans Seliman - antiques dealer.

A later article read:

Regarding the rash of jewel heists, some of the jewelry was recovered by way of the black market. The valuable Blue Dolphins, several antique bracelets, a genuine eighteenth-century silver clover locket, and a rare Victorian emerald pin have yet to be recovered.

Those words struck me like a knife. Could I have been misguided all along? Was it possible?

On my way home I made a quick stop at the hardware store to pick up a new collar and leash for Paw. He could be rough on them with all his weight and energy pulling when he lunged.

No one appeared to be home as I walked in the front door. On the table in the hall, a package with my name on it sat amongst the rest of the mail. I picked it up and went to my room. In my room I looked over the package; it was covered with standard brown paper and had no return address.

I opened the package to discover a box of Claudette's chocolates. These were my favorite candies when I was a child. However, I had not eaten chocolate for a while because of doctor's orders.

The next thing I knew Paw jumped up, knocked the chocolates out of my hands, grabbed the box, and dumped it in the trash can. He was clearly telling me not to eat the candy. Paw knows he can't have chocolate, but I'd never seen him throw something in the trash. Oddly, as I went to retrieve them, he growled and pushed me away. That's when I became truly suspicious that something was wrong with the chocolates.

I reexamined the wrapper but could not find any return address. That is when I realized that the chocolates hadn't been mailed. There was no postage stamped on the package. Now how did it get in with the mail?

I decided to take the chocolates and the wrapper to the local police. Hopefully, they would take my concerns seriously. The sergeant at the front desk listened carefully. He took the chocolates and the wrapper and wrote up a report. They would be sent off to a lab for testing. The only problem was that it could take weeks at the earliest for the test results to come back. He advised me to be careful and report any further incidents.

Sighing, I left the police station.

It wasn't that they didn't want to help. The police were just too busy. Now I had time to worry if I was in any danger. After all, Paw could have just been trying to keep me from eating chocolate.

As I stood thinking, I glanced across the street and did a double take. Hiram, an old friend of mine, stood photographing something on the sidewalk. I crossed the street to talk to him.

"Hiram, is that you?" I waved at him.

He jerked his head up. Smiling, he laughed, "Clarissa, my love, how are you? Come see what I have found." He gestured to a small dot on the sidewalk. It turned out to be a ladybug.

"A ladybug. How lovely. I didn't know you were into photography. I thought you were all about science."

"That is Camille's doing." Camille was Hiram's girlfriend and a friend of mine as well. "She says I spend too much time in the lab. She's tired of hearing about chemical reac-

A Dog Detective Short Story Collection

tions and Bunsen burners. So she *suggested* that I get a hobby. So here I am taking photos of bugs." He laughed again good-naturedly. "What are you doing here?"

"I am visiting a cousin of mine. How about you?"

"A chemist's conference. Camille hates them, so I'm here by myself. Hey, how about we have dinner tonight and catch up?"

"That sounds great! There is a restaurant on Goode Street called the Rusty Wren. How about we meet there at 6 PM?" I smiled.

"I'll see you then." As we had talked, his ladybug had flown away. Shrugging, he gave me a little wave and went back to looking for photographic ideas.

Paw was stretched out on the bed when I returned to Lucinda's. I told him about seeing Hiram. He immediately sat up. Hiram was one of his favorite people. Maybe because he and Hiram both loved bacon sandwiches and Hiram would share his with Paw.

I decided to take a bath. I pondered what could be in those chocolates while I was soaking in the tub. Truthfully, I was glad to eat out tonight. Those candies showing up here was a little too close for comfort. Just then I realized how stupid I was. Hiram was a chemist. He probably could have tested those candies and gotten quick results. I wish I had known Hiram was in town before I took the chocolates to the police. Who knew how long it would take the police to get the chocolates tested?

I finished my bath and went to get dressed. That's when I noticed Paw bat a round object from under the bed. Curious, I picked it up. Paw looked at me expectantly. It was a chocolate candy like the ones I took to the police. I must have missed one when I gathered them out of the trash.

"Paw, you are brilliant." I hugged him. "I'll take this tonight and ask Hiram to test it."

The Rusty Wren was a charming little restaurant that served seafood from the local fishermen. Hiram was waiting for me at a table. After quick hellos, we both ordered the seafood special - seafood chowder and steamed veggies. While we waited for our food, I told Hiram about the chocolates.

"This is serious, Clarissa. You could be in danger." Hiram shook his head.

"I know, Hiram. That's why I went to the police, but I hate waiting to find out if those candies were poisoned. Do you have your equipment with you? Could you test this one?" I pulled out the chocolate I had placed in a tissue.

"Of course, Clarissa. I always have my equipment. Even better, the conference provided lab space for us to use. We'll go over there right after dinner and test it."

We chatted about old times through our meal, then paid and went over to the conference lab. I didn't know much about chemistry so I sat back and let Hiram work. It took a few hours, but then Hiram turned to me with a serious expression.

"Cyanide. The chocolate is laced with it."

I paled even though I had suspected something was wrong. "Hiram, will the police listen to you? Will they believe your results?"

"Yes, they should. Besides, I am friends with Dr. Evans. He is in charge of the lab that the police use. You want to take this to them I assume?"

"Yes, the sooner, the better."

He nodded, turned around, and went to the phone to call Dr. Evans.

We met Dr. Evans at the police station. He arranged with the sergeant to test some of the chocolates the police had. The sergeant accompanied us to the lab. A few more hours and we knew all the chocolates were laced with cyanide. That is when the sergeant began to listen to me and a plan I had formulated. The sergeant agreed to speak with the one person I felt could answer a few of his questions then we planned the trap.

One of the police officers, calling anonymously, contacted each person on my list. He told each one if they wanted the Blue Dolphins to meet him at the mill at midnight.

That night Sergeant Blackwell, five officers, myself, and Paw waited at the mill. We concealed ourselves in a cluster of trees to the right side of the mill within sight of the mill's front door. I hugged Paw close to me to keep him quiet.

Our first suspect soon arrived.

Father Henry.

He walked to the mill's front door and turned the handle. He twisted and pulled, but the door was locked. Slumping his shoulders, he leaned against the wall.

Sergeant Blackwell shifted next to me.

I heard footsteps and our second suspect arrived.

Aunt Mavis.

She scanned the area as she approached Father Henry.

"Did the caller show up?" she asked him.

"No."

Someone else was approaching.

Lucinda stepped out of the trees to my left. She walked past our hiding place, ignoring us.

I hoped she wasn't involved in these thefts.

Lucinda walked up to Father Henry and Mavis. "Did the caller show? Did you get the Blue Dolphins?"

Mavis scowled. "I just got here. According to him," she nodded to Father Henry, "no one has shown up."

Father Henry growled, "That's because no one *has* shown up."

Mavis crossed her arms and glared at Lucinda. "What are you doing here? We agreed that only one of us would meet the caller."

Lucinda smirked. "Like I would trust either of you. Besides, I can get more info out of the guy than either of you. We need to find out what my foolish uncle did with those diamonds."

So she was involved in the thefts.

Sergeant Blackwell and his officers stepped from concealment and surrounded the group by the mill.

Paw and I followed.

Lucinda stared at me in disgust. "I knew your visit was a mistake. You just have to play detective, don't you?"

Paw growled at her.

A Dog Detective Short Story Collection

Sergeant Blackwell held Lucinda by her right arm. "It's a good thing she did."

He nodded to me. "Why don't you explain, Ms. Hayes?"

I tucked a strand of hair behind my ear and began.

"You see it all started four years ago. Aunt Mavis and Father Henry met up with Hans Seliman. They decided to form an association and begin robbing jewelry stores. However, they needed a point person. Lucinda was perfect for the job. She was beautiful and intelligent. Plus, she knew Hans through their antiques connection."

Sergeant Blackwell interrupted, "What about Josh? Was he involved?"

I shook my head. "No. I'm pretty sure they kept him in the dark."

Blackwell motioned for me to continue.

"Anyway, the robberies were successful until the last one when Hans was killed. After that, they had to lie low.

"But somehow Uncle Josh found out about the robberies. He must have found the missing jewels and red dress."

Sergeant Blackwell shook his head. "How can you know that?"

I held up my hand. "I'll explain in a minute."

The Sergeant nodded in agreement.

I continued, "My guess is that he confronted Lucinda. He may have thought she was an unwilling pawn. He loved her and probably couldn't believe she would willingly commit a crime.

"Maybe she lied to him. She confessed to making a

horrible mistake but begged him to help her. She was in over her head. So he covered up for her so that Mavis and Father Henry couldn't blackmail her later. He buried the red dress that Paw found in the garden. Then he hid the jewels.

"He couldn't turn Mavis or Father Henry into the police for fear of exposing Lucinda. Perhaps he confronted Mavis about the jewels and dress. He probably told her he was cleaning up their mess and was furious with her for involving Lucinda. Mavis would have known the jewels that Josh hid were missing from where she had hidden them.

"But something went wrong. Either Mavis or Father Henry resented Josh's involvement. One of them poisoned him."

I turned to glare at them.

"Just as I would have been poisoned with the chocolates if it weren't for Paw. Someone tried to warn me when I first arrived. Nellie... I think was the one who left the note under my door... had suspicions all along about what had happened to Josh, but was too scared to go to the police."

Lucinda asked incredulously, "How did you know I was involved in the robberies?"

"First was the silver locket you were wearing when I arrived. It didn't mean anything until I read the newspaper article stating an eighteenth-century silver clover locket was missing.

"Secondly, few people knew I loved Claudette's chocolates as a young child. You knew. That was before you moved in with Uncle Josh and Aunt Mavis – they wouldn't

A Dog Detective Short Story Collection

have known. Luckily for me, I never told anybody about my doctor's orders not to eat chocolate."

I crossed my arms over my chest and shook my head. "There's just one thing I don't understand. How could you..."

The words burst out of Lucinda as if she was relieved to be free of the guilt. "They didn't poison him – I did! He kept trying to convince me to move away. To start a new life away from Mavis and Henry." She scoffed. "As if I wanted the thefts to end! I was eager to get them started up again!"

Sergeant Blackwell nodded to me. "So where are these Blue Dolphins?"

"Right where Josh safely left them," I said as I reached down to Paw. "I checked at the hardware store; this collar has no attachment. Josh made one to store the earrings." As I said this, I opened the pouch.

Out slid two sparkling sapphire earrings.

The Sergeant said, "Ok, boys, take 'em away."

The sergeant turned to me and smiled. "Thank you for all your help. We might never have realized it was this trio if you hadn't put the clues together." He dropped to one knee. "And thanks to you, Paw. You were a loyal friend to keep your mistress safe from harm."

Paw responded in the way he knew best. He licked the sergeant full across the face.

2

THE MYSTERY OF AUNT CAROL'S DISAPPEARANCE

1990s

The rain pelted the windshield as though it had a personal vengeance against the world. I was in the front passenger seat trying to distinguish our location through barely visible road signs. Jacqueline was driving slowly. Unusual since her usual motto was fast and faster. We were supposed to be on a fun-filled sunny vacation to a relative's beach house. So far though it hadn't been fun nor relaxing.

The problems started before we even got in the car.

Paw had jumped in the car and sat in the front passenger seat, but I needed to sit there and navigate for Jac. I couldn't have a Saint Bernard on my lap. I grasped his collar, tugging him from the car.

When I tried to push him into the back seat, Shelbee

balked. "I refuse to sit next to him. Clarissa, you know I love animals, but Paw is huge. It will take hours to get there and Paw always hogs the seat."

Finally we compromised.

I climbed into the back seat with Shelbee. "I promise he'll behave. Here's a bag of dog toys. They'll keep him entertained."

She nodded her agreement, albeit reluctantly.

I climbed out and bribed Paw with a doggy bone to sit in the back. He jumped in, eager for his treat.

We started our trip.

Now after three hours, one flat tire, two roadblocks, and a half hour wait, we were stuck. Visibility was zero and everyone was tense. That's when Paw decided to honor us with his wonderful voice of woofs. Apparently he had seen something.

I sighed. "Oh, drat. He must have seen a cat!"

Anyway, as I turned to look I saw a large sign. It read: "Welcome to Happyville. Pop. 957."

"Yes! Finally we're here." I gave Paw a hug over the seat back. Perhaps it was coincidence, but I believe my St. Bernard is not only highly intelligent but also a little psychic.

Jac exhaled, brushing her black hair out of her eyes. "Well, it's about time. I'll be glad to get outta this car." Jac is her nickname. Her full name is Jacqueline Marie Weldon. She's a blue-eyed, five-foot-six health nut who loves tofu.

Shelb laughed saying, "I can't wait to eat. It's been at least two hours since we stopped." Katrina Shelbee Van Vight even gave Paw a hug. She hated the name Katrina so we called her Shelb. With her bright red hair, green eyes, and slim figure, she could easily be a model.

By the way, my name is Clarissa Montgomery Hayes. I'm the short one of the group at five-foot-two. With my blonde hair and hazel eyes, I look sweet, but once people get to know me they find out how strong-willed I can be. Jac and Shelb are my two closest friends. We all needed a break from work and when Jac's Aunt Carol offered the beach house we jumped at the chance. I was concerned that I wouldn't be able to take Paw. But Carol said it would be fine; she loved dogs. Paudius Pernivious — Paw, for short — went everywhere with me. He was a great companion and a good watchdog. Good meaning he was more likely to slobber you than growl at you.

Stepping into the pouring rain, I heard the waves of the ocean crashing. The water, choppy and foamy, seemed to dance an insane waltz with the beach. Paw, who delighted in trouble, started for the sand. I called to him but got no response. Fortunately, I caught up with him quickly.

I went back to the car to get my luggage. Pulling Paw with one hand and dragging a suitcase in the other, I reached the house. It was a small cottage appearing to have been built many years ago. The house had been painted a creamy white with a slate blue roof. Paint had chipped away from years of weathered abuse.

"Where's the key?" Shelbee yelled. "I'm drenched."

"Aunt Carol said she'd leave it open," Jac exclaimed. But the door was locked and wouldn't budge.

I suggested, "Maybe she left a key. Look around!" After a lengthy search Jac found it under a nearby flower pot. She inserted the key and flung the door open. Paw, a self-defined king, entered to investigate his new domain.

We changed clothes, made dinner, and curled up in front of a blazing fire. Paw had claimed the warmest spot and with his stomach full, fell fast asleep.

Jacqueline sighed. "It sure feels good to be warm and dry. I thought we'd never make it here. So what are we going to do on our vacation?"

I thought about how Paw and I both love nature. "In the morning, I'm going to take a walk on the beach. Maybe check out the seagulls and other creatures in the sand. You know they have a fantastic aquarium and I've heard there's a wonderful restaurant in town."

Shelbee's eyes lit up. "Well, all I plan to do is lie on the beach and get tanned. And while I'm doing that who knows I might meet a cute guy."

I yawned. "I'm going to bed. I'll see you guys in the morning. Goodnight."

"Sleep well."

After changing to my nightgown, I went to shut the blinds. To my surprise I saw flashing yellow lights at sea.

Now who on earth would be out on a night like this.

Then the lights quickly vanished and the sea roiled with waves.

I shook my head.

I must be imaging things. Probably too tired.

I closed the blinds and slept peacefully all night long.

The next morning, I woke up, opening the blinds to bright beautiful sunshine. The clock read 11am – we had all slept late after the exhausting drive in the rain. I dressed and went down to breakfast. Jacqueline and Shelbee weren't up yet so I decided to treat us all to pancakes for brunch. As the pan warmed I became aware of a scratching sound. I looked over at the living room and found Paw scratching the carpet under the coffee table.

"PAUDIUS PERNIVIOUS! Stop that scratching! You're going to ruin the carpet and we're guests here. You should be on good behavior." I took Paw to the patio door. He, reluctantly, went out and was soon rolling on the beach.

Jac came downstairs. "What was that all about?"

"Sometimes he gets upset with a new place. He probably just needed to go out. Take a look! He's having a great time on the beach."

Shelb cried with delight. "I smell pancakes. I looove pancakes."

I smiled. "Everybody sit down. They're almost done."

Shelb got the syrup. "That's okay, we'll help."

Jac got the plates and silverware.

We dug into the pancakes and stuffed ourselves. I had forgotten all about Paw until I saw him running to the house. I should have known he was having too much fun. Before he even got in the door, we could smell it.

Shelb and Jac cried in unison. "Paw; UCK, gross."

I coughed. "Oh Paw. You sure do stink. I should have known you would retaliate." He stood there panting with a blissful look on his face. He had rolled in dead fish and he stunk so bad my eyes watered.

I pointed a finger at him. "I guess my walk on the beach is out. It's a bath for you, mister."

He looked sorrowful with his droopy eyes, but I knew he was smiling inside.

Our bath took two hours. By the time I had washed Paw three times, he was smelling fresh and clean, much to his dislike. When washing Paw I always get soaked. He'll stand up and shake off, sending water from here to China. That's his favorite part. After I cleaned the bathroom and changed to dry clothes, Paw and I went for a walk.

"Ok, Paw. We still have a few hours before dusk. But this time you're going to wear your leash." He waved his tail happily, anticipating another "fishy" outing. This time I vowed he wouldn't make it.

We walked slowly enjoying the late afternoon sun. The ocean was calm with light waves gently lapping the beach. Three children were building a sand castle. When they saw Paw they dropped their pails and came running.

"He's neat!" The little girl said. I guessed she was six years old.

The older boy commanded. "Stay back Sarah. You, too, Henry. He might bite." Henry, perhaps seven, drooped his head looking sad.

I smiled. "It's all right. He doesn't bite. You can pet him."

Henry asked, "What kind of dog is he? What's his name?"

Sarah asked, "How old is he?"

The older boy, Mike, chimed in, "I like him. He's very soft."

By now all three were petting him.

"His name is Paw. He's a St. Bernard. They are very lovable, playful dogs. Paw is two years old."

Mike gave Paw a final pat. "Henry, Sarah. We gotta go now. Mom's expectin' us."

Both gave Paw a farewell pat and ran toward a green beach house. Paw and I continued on our walk. Suddenly Paw jerked on the leash, heading for the ocean. Before I could react he stopped and began furiously digging in the sand. Paw got his nickname because he loves to dig.

I trudged through the sand to his side. Something glimmered on the sand by Paw's foot. I bent over and picked it up. It was a ring. I turned it over in my hand, brushing sand off it.

As the sand fell off, a diamond solitaire set in a silver band was revealed. I examined the ring closely. Engraved on the inside of the band was an inscription:

TO CMJ FROM RPJ.

Curious, I thought. Whoever lost it would surely want it back. I pocketed the ring with the goal to take it to the lost and found at the lifeguard station in the morning.

It was getting late so Paw and I walked home. Shelb had made dinner— fresh catfish with fried potatoes and carrots. We finished supper, cleaned the dishes, and settled down in the living room to discuss our first day.

Shelb said, "There are a lot of cute guys on the beach. I met one who said he is a lifeguard. His name is Steve. He has blond hair and blue eyes. Besides that I got started on a great tan."

"Yes. You do look more tanned," I said. "Well, as far as my day went, I got soaked bathing Paudius and then we took a walk. The only guys I saw were six and ten years old. And their five year old sister. They were building a sand castle."

"Kids are cute. I checked out that restaurant you mentioned 'Rissa." 'Rissa's my nickname. Jac went on, "It has great food. Then I did a little shopping. There are good bargains and there's a drive-in movie theater. You don't see those nowadays."

When she stopped talking all of us noticed a scratching noise. Paw was under the coffee table again.

"Stop that!" I yelled. Paw laid down; putting his head on his paws, he tried to look innocent.

Jac laughed. "Maybe he's digging for buried treasure."

"Hey. Speaking of treasure, Paw found this on the beach today." I withdrew the ring from my pocket and handed it to Jacqueline.

Shelbee exclaimed, "Ooh. Pretty."

I pointed. "Read the inscription."

As Jac read the initials her eyes widened. "This is Aunt Carol's wedding ring!"

Shelbee asked, "Are you sure?"

Jac cried, "Of course, I'm sure. I adored it ever since I was little. She'd never go anywhere without it."

I tapped my lips. "Then maybe we better check that your Aunt Carol is all right."

Jacqueline immediately stood and went into the kitchen to call her Aunt Selma. Aunt Carol was supposed to be staying with Selma for a few weeks. We overheard Jac's conversation. By the tone in her voice, something was wrong. When she returned to the living room, her brow was furrowed with concern.

"Aunt Carol never arrived." Jac, dismayed, dropped into her chair. "Aunt Selma says she and Aunt Carol were originally going to meet four days ago. But the plan changed when Selma had to travel the first few days for work. She told Carol to come at the original time and stay at her house alone for a few days. Aunt Selma assumed Aunt Carol had changed her mind about visiting."

"Maybe she decided to do some sightseeing before she got to your Aunt Selma's house," Shelbee consoled.

Jac firmly shook her head. "No. Once Aunt Carol started to travel, she drove straight to a destination, and if she encountered a problem, she called for help."

I leaned forward. "In that case we better file a missing person's report. Also, we can ask the neighbors if they saw her lately or if they saw anything strange."

Jac jumped up, saying, "I'll call the police right now."

From the kitchen, we could hear Jac say, "I want to report my aunt missing."

There was a pause, then, "Yes. She's been missing for four days. Her name is – "

As Jac covered the basics with the police, I motioned to Shelbee that I was taking Paw for a walk before bed.

The night was calm, but I was not. *What happened to Aunt Carol?*

Where was she and what could we do about it?

Paw finished his business and we returned to the house.

As I entered the living room, Jac returned from the kitchen.

Jac began pacing. "The police want me to come to the station tomorrow to answer more questions and to bring photos of Aunt Carol. But I want to do something now. Who knows what could be happening to her?"

Shelbee stood up, walked over to Jac, and hugged her. "You know we'll help you anyway we can. Why don't we choose some photos of your aunt to show the police?"

I hung up Paw's leash. "I agree. We can question the neighbors in the morning when people are awake. Plus, Shelbee and I can take a photo and show it to the neighbors."

Jac nodded reluctantly. She pulled down three photo albums from the bookcase.

She and Shelbee scanned the albums for suitable photos.

While they selected photos, I checked that all the doors and windows were locked downstairs. Once everything was secure, I joined the photo search.

Shelbee held up a photo. "What about this one?"

I took it from her. "This is a good shot. It shows her face clearly."

Jac closed the album she was scanning. "That should do it. We already have four more photos. You each can take one and I'll take the other three to the station."

Shelbee nodded in agreement.

I stood up. "Good. Now I think we all should get some sleep."

Jac replaced the albums. "I don't think I can sleep."

Shelbee patted her back. "Just try."

The three of us, plus Paw, went upstairs.

Paw and I went into our room. I closed my window, looking out across the ocean. There was a light breeze, but otherwise the water was calm. This time I saw no lights.

I slept fitfully. I dreamed of Aunt Carol trapped in a small room. Tables were everywhere. There were flashing lights all around me. Then the scene changed to a small boat on a pond. Suddenly, wind began to roar and water splashed everywhere. I felt like I was being smothered.

I woke suddenly. It took me a minute to assess my surroundings. That's when I realized the weather had changed. Rain slashed at the house as thunderstorms moved across the sky. As far as the smothering that I dreamed, well I soon found the reason for that. Paw was lying right up against me. He hated thunderstorms and had taken refuge in my bed. I went back to sleep and didn't wake until morning.

The day began with light rain. It was a Thursday. The rain wasn't a problem but it made the tasks ahead miserable.

After breakfast Jac went to the police station to follow up on the missing person's report. Shelb and I planned to meet her at the local café for lunch. Since it was raining, we donned raincoats in preparation for interviewing the neighbors. I left Paw at the house when he balked at going out in the rain. Dogs!

Shelbee and I stepped out into a steady drizzle. We split up. Shelbee planned to interview the neighbors to the right of Carol's house. I went left.

I knocked on the door of the first house I came to. No one answered. I'd try again on my way back.

A fashionably-dressed woman answered the door to the second house.

I smiled politely. "Good morning. My name is Clarissa Hayes. I am staying at my friend's aunt's house two doors down. Carol Jackson." I held up Carol's photo. "Do you know her?"

The woman opened the door wider. She glanced at the photo. "Yes, I do. Won't you come in?"

I hesitated. "Thank you for the invitation, but I really am in a hurry. I wonder if you remember when you last saw Carol."

She frowned. "Why do you want to know? Surely, Carol can tell you when she last saw me."

I explained, "Carol is missing. She was to have arrived at her sister's four days ago. We just found out she never arrived and are worried about her. Is there anything you could tell me to help find her?"

The woman crossed her arms. "Let me think. I suppose it was a few weeks ago. We both attended the new art museum exhibition. They have a lovely collection of decorative vases. I collect decorative vases. Would you like to see them?"

"No, thank you. So you haven't seen her more recently?"

"No."

I backed from the door. "Thank you for your help."

I moved to the next house. It was painted light yellow with dark blue shutters.

I rang the doorbell.

A short man with thinning hair answered the door. "I'm not interested in anything you're selling." He began to close the door.

I put my hand out to push at the door. "Wait. I'm not selling anything. I'm asking the neighbors if they have seen my friend's aunt, Carol Jackson." I showed him Carol's photo. "She lives in the white house with the blue shutters. She's missing and we are worried."

The man scowled, not even looking at the photo. "Don't know her. Now go away."

He slammed the door in my face.

Cursing under my breath, I trudged to the last house and knocked on the door.

I waited, pulling my raincoat hood closer around my head. The rain was increasing. Another minute and I gave up and walked back the way I had come.

I passed the houses where I had interviewed the man and woman. Stopping in front of the first house, I approached it again. Maybe someone was home now.

I walked up to the door and knocked.

The door was opened by a tall man. He had a thick head of brown hair turning silver.

He spoke with a well-cultured voice. "Can I help you?"

I plastered on a smile. "Yes. Do you know Carol Jackson? She lives next door to you." I nodded my head toward her house and held up her photo.

He hesitated. "And who are you?"

I realized in my impatience that I hadn't introduced myself. "My name is Clarissa Hayes. I'm friends with her niece. Carol is missing and we're hoping to find out where she is. Have you seen her recently?"

He raised an eyebrow. "Missing? That's terrible." He stroked his chin. "Let me think. The last time I saw her was on the beach last Thursday."

My hopes rose. "What was she doing?"

He checked his watch. "She was collecting sand in a pail. I teased her that she was an adult not a child."

He looked at his watch again. "I really have to go. I have an appointment. Keep me informed about Carol. I consider her a friend."

I put out my hand. "Thank you for your help, Mr...er..."

He shook my hand. "Phillips."

I released his hand and he closed the door.

As I walked back to Aunt Carol's house, I wondered if Mr. Phillips had told me everything he knew. He was in a hurry to get rid of me if checking his watch was any indication. If he had an appointment, why wasn't he at his house when I knocked the first time? Perhaps he had been in the shower.

I stepped up on Carol's front porch and threw back my hood. Shelbee walked toward me. She wore a dejected expression.

I waited to greet her until she stepped onto the porch. "Hey. Any luck?"

Shelbee huffed. "No. That was a complete waste of time. How about you?"

I smiled. "I had a little luck." I related my experiences.

Shelbee shook her head. "You did a lot better than me. I only spoke with one person. She was a nice old lady with a houseful of cats. I love cats and she had a beautiful Persian, but all she wanted to talk about was the cats. She didn't recognize Carol's photo either."

I tilted my head on the side to stretch my neck. "What about the other houses?"

She sighed. "No one answered at the other houses. Maybe we can try them later."

I straightened my neck and put up my hood. "Let's go to the café. Maybe Jac had better luck."

Jac was waiting for us. "I filed the report, but the police weren't very hopeful." She fought back tears. "Please tell me one of you had luck."

Shelbee and I hugged her.

We broke apart when a waitress arrived with menus and glasses of water. She took our orders and hurried away.

Shelbee pushed her menu aside. "I wish I had better news." She recounted her experiences of the morning.

Jac hung her head.

I took a sip of water. "I have better news." I relayed the two interviews that had been helpful.

Jac nodded. "I remember Aunt Carol mentioning Mr.

Phillips. He's been her neighbor for several years. I just wish he could have told us more."

Shelbee opened her menu. "You need to eat. We all do. Perhaps it will help us think of a new plan."

We placed our orders. I chose a tuna sandwich and chips. Shelbee wanted a salad with chicken strips while Jac only ordered a small salad.

We sat in silence, each lost in our own thoughts until our food arrived.

Before the waitress left, I showed her Carol's picture. "Have you seen this woman lately?"

The waitress stared at the photo. "I've seen her in here a few times."

Jac raised her head. "When was the last time you saw her?"

The waitress fidgeted with her order pad and pencil. "I'd say a week ago."

I asked, "Was anyone with her?"

The waitress tapped her pen on the tabletop. "No. Not that I remember."

Jac's expression fell. "Thanks."

The waitress nodded before turning to another table.

Jac picked at her salad while Shelbee and I devoured our food.

Outside the rain continued to pour. Very few people were out and about.

Once we finished our lunch, we agreed to spend the afternoon at the house, in case someone called with news about Aunt Carol.

A Dog Detective Short Story Collection

Once we got there we each went to complete different tasks. Jac was going to call her dad to inform him of her Aunt Carol's disappearance. Shelbee was going to do some postcard writing and I was going to write a short article on the beach. Being a freelance writer my topics varied depending on where I was staying. The magazine I wrote for thought a piece on life at the beach would be great to boost summer sales.

Jac, Shelb, and I had just come into the living room when Paw started scratching under the coffee table again. This time I went over, grabbed him by the collar, and took him to the patio door.

"If you want to scratch go outside!" It was still raining and, therefore, Paw refused to go out. Instead he sat down and would not move.

I shrugged. "Okay, stay there."

Returning to the room, I went over to the coffee table to check the carpet. There was a frayed streak in the strands of the carpet.

"Oh, Paw. Now look what you did. Aunt Carol will be..." I stopped talking. Everyone turned to look at me.

"'Rissa, you all right?" Jac and Shelb asked in unison.

"I don't believe how stupid I've been. Paw I apologize. You knew what you were doing all along." I stared at the carpet, totally dismayed.

Shelb and Jac stared at me with worried expressions.

I pointed. "I was touching the fray when I noticed a crack in the floor. I found that it continued for a good eight inches."

Shelb and Jac continued to stare blankly.

I crouched next to it. "Don't you see? It's a trap door. Come help me lift the coffee table away."

They did just that. After the table was moved, we could easily pick out the edges of the trap door. It had been cleverly covered with carpet making the whole floor resemble a normal wall-to-wall carpeting. We lifted the door and found a small storage space. Hidden in it were papers and a few photographs.

Jac, Shelb, and I divided up the photos and papers. We each read quietly for a few minutes. Then we compared notes.

Shelbee handed a picture to me. "Take a look at this photo. It looks like a ship. The picture's so dark I can't be sure."

Jac nodded. "Yeah. There's a ship in this photo, too. And these papers are about toxic waste and smuggling!"

I put out a hand. "Let me see all the photos." I laid all the pictures side by side; there were five of them. "Yes, this is definitely a ship. Wait a minute! Look at this one. There's a boat next to the ship and it appears to be loading something!" I handed the photo to Shelb and Jac.

Jac examined the photo. "I agree. It looks like something being loaded.

I cried, "Now my dream is making sense."

Jac looked at me. "What dream?"

I described my dream to them. "The tables must have meant the coffee table. And the boat was the ship with the

A Dog Detective Short Story Collection

other boat next to it. Of course! I saw the flashing lights the first night we arrived here."

"Flashing lights?!" Shelbee asked in surprise. I described the lights to her.

Jac sighed. "Aunt Carol must have gotten herself into real trouble. She wrote me about dead fish and the ocean being poisoned. She loves the ocean and would do anything to protect it."

Shelbee's brow furrowed. "I saw a lot of dead fish on the beach. I thought it had to do with the storm."

"You remember, Paw rolled in dead fish and I had to bathe him. Paw," I hugged him, "you knew things were wrong, didn't you?" He rolled his eyes and smiled at me.

"Ok," I began. "Suppose this ship is smuggling in toxic waste — no, more likely some kind of chemicals — and signaling for delivery with those flashing lights. Then the boat goes out, picks up the stuff, and brings it to shore."

"That makes sense," Shelb said.

Jac asked, "Yeah, but what caused the poisoning?"

I shrugged. "Maybe on one of the routine pick-ups chemicals accidently spilled into the water. The fish died and washed up on shore. Aunt Carol was suspicious so she began to investigate. Somehow the smugglers found out. Maybe they kidnapped her and she lost her wedding ring in a struggle with them."

"Oh, no," Jac sobbed. "Suppose she's dead."

"No, I don't think she is. They probably know she has info on them and want it back, but they don't know where it is. In fact, we wouldn't have found it if it weren't for Paw."

Paw jumped up, barked in agreement, and licked Jac's face.

Shelb turned to me. "So what do we do, 'Rissa?"

"Well, we can go to the police with what evidence we have. Aunt Carol only wrote down one date – Tues., a week ago - so we don't know how often they come. We also don't know what the return signal is. The police can keep patrols out if they believe what we tell them."

Jac began gathering the photos and papers into a folder. "Let's go now."

Full of determination we set out. It had stopped raining. We stopped at the library first to make copies of the photos and papers, then trooped to the police station.

The sergeant on duty listened half-heartedly to our explanation and took our documents, placing them in a manila envelope. "I'll look at your documents as soon as I can." He plopped the envelope onto a tall stack of papers on his desk.

A clerk called to him. "Sergeant Gray, your wife's on the line again."

With a grunt, the sergeant waved us away and picked up his phone.

Dragging our feet, we left the police station and went home.

Once home, Jac dropped into a chair at the kitchen table. "There must be something more we can do."

Shelbee spread out our document copies on the table. "Let's look at these again."

We pored over the photos and papers again.

A Dog Detective Short Story Collection

Jac rubbed her eyes. "My eyes are killing me."

I yawned and stretched. "We need to take a break. Come back to it when we're fresh. Why don't the two of you go to a movie? Get your mind off things."

Jac protested, "I can't enjoy myself when Aunt Carol could be in danger."

Shelbee stood up. "'Rissa's right. We need a break. If we see a movie, I bet we'll come back to this with a clearer mind."

Reluctantly, Jac stood up. "All right." She looked at me. "You coming?"

I shook my head. "You two go. I'll stay with Paw. We'll regroup in a few hours."

They nodded and I soon had the house to myself.

I got up and went to make a cup of tea. I had just finished when Paw started barking. He led me to the patio. Across the ocean a pale yellow light flashed. I grabbed the binoculars; yes, the signal. Panning across the beach I found the return signal. Of course! The movie theater spotlight. A very clever signal.

I rushed to the phone and dialed the police. Ring...Ring...Ring...

I didn't have time to wait. I wrote a quick note to the girls, grabbed a sweater, and flashlight, and telling Paw he had to stay, shut the patio door.

I moved at a brisk pace over the beach. I had to find where the shipment came onto shore. The breeze grew sharper in the darkening evening. I was glad I had put on a sweater.

I had just crawled over a small sand dune when I saw them. A mid-sized rowboat, maybe fifteen feet with a canvas-covered front, rocked gently in the waves. Ten yards away two men stood arguing with their backs to me.

Cautiously I crawled across the beach to the boat. Once on the boat I stayed low. Searching for clues I found nothing. Just as I was going to get off, the men began coming in my direction. They were still arguing.

I had just enough time to hide under a nearby canvas. I could see the men through a small hole in the canvas though.

"Okay, okay. We'll do it your way. But I still don't like it," the first man said as he boarded the boat. He was five-foot-nine with burly shoulders and cropped black hair.

"Trust me," the second soothed as he too boarded. "I know what I'm doing." He was young, early twenties, with jet-black hair. Taller than the other man he had a square-set jaw. "Let's get going."

"Yeah, right." The burly man reached for the canvas. "But first I want to check that we got everything."

Now I realized that I had been lying on a pile of rope. Other items were there, too, but I didn't have time to identify them. I was doomed. There was no other place to hide and soon they'd see me.

That's when I heard a "Woof! Woof!" I'd know that voice anywhere. Somehow Paw had got out and followed me. I heard the burly man say "What's that?" as he dropped the canvas.

Paw jumped into the boat.

Apparently, one man, burly, had grabbed Paw's collar because I heard him say, "Dang dog won't budge. What 'n we do now, Jack?"

Jack had a well-cultured voice."Let him stay. We're late as it is. Let's get started."

The boat shoved off and within five minutes we had reached the ship. The two tied up the boat and made their way up a flight of metal stairs connected to the side of the ship. Paw was left with me. Cautiously, I peeked out from under cover. All was clear. I hugged Paw and we quietly climbed the steps. To my left were stacks of barrels. The bridge was above me and on my right five men stood talking. The two from the boat, the captain and first mate from the ship, and another man with bulging muscles.

"Now what?" I whispered to Paw.

He headed toward the barrels. They were each labeled with white stickers. The stickers read: Grain – DO NOT OPEN. I seriously doubted the barrels contained grain. However, they were sealed too tight for me to open. I did remove a label for evidence. If I could get to the police in time, they could arrest these guys.

But how would I delay them? Where was Aunt Carol?

Paw found the trap door to the hold and down we went. I checked every room while Paw kept lookout. No Aunt Carol.

That's when I saw the toolbox. I took out a large wrench and headed back to the engine room. I sent a silent thank you to my cousin, Ben. Thankfully, I had spent several summers helping him work on his boat and learned a lot about boat engines. You could say I put a "wrench in their plans."

After disabling the engine, I knew they weren't going anywhere for a while.

Paw and I headed up through the trap door. As I eased onto the deck, I heard voices coming in our direction.

Jack and a short man with a lopsided cap were walking toward my location. Two large men followed behind them.

The short one was saying, "We should leave immediately. Can't tell when the weather might change for the worse."

Jack snapped, "I'm the one in charge. I decide when we leave."

Paw and I had less than ten seconds before the men saw us.

Heart pounding, I scanned my surroundings. Behind me was a short flight of steps which I assumed led to the bridge. I tugged on Paw's collar and we sprinted up the steps.

The door to the bridge room was open and we dashed inside. I eased the door closed and locked it.

My heart was racing.

I crouched next to Paw and scratched his ears. "Stay quiet, buddy."

I eased over to the windshield above the bridge control panel and peeked out.

The men were still in conversation as they began to climb the steps.

I crawled back to Paw and we huddled under the door's small window, out of sight.

Hopefully, no one would attempt to come onto the bridge.

The men's voices grew louder then fainter as they passed the bridge and moved on.

I realized I was holding my breath and exhaled in relief.

While I sat on the floor taking deep breaths, I scanned the bridge. It was small with a control panel in front and a counter on the back wall.

I had a sudden thought. *Did the captain keep a ship's log?* If so, it could provide further evidence of the smuggling operation to get the police's attention.

I cautiously stood up and checked the windows. No one was in sight.

Paw stood up, tail wagging.

I whispered reassurances to him. "It's okay. You're doing great. Just stay quiet a little longer."

His tongue lolled out and he sat down.

I eased over to the counter. It was covered in papers, empty plastic coffee cups, scrunched up napkins, and an open map. I shuffled through the mess, hoping to find a log book. I glanced briefly at the map. It displayed the coast of this area, but nothing was marked on it. I moved the map aside to look under it. Nothing.

I pushed aside papers. My hand brushed against a book-like object. I pulled it out from under the sprawled papers. It was the size of a small paperback book with a leather cover and words stamped into it:

Ship's log.

I did a little jig.

With the log in one hand and grasping Paw's collar in the other, we climbed down from the bridge on the other side. Across from us the metal steps led down to the boat. All we had to do was jump on the boat and speed away, get the police, and arrest these smugglers.

As I headed for the steps, Paw tugged from my grasp.

"Hold it!" A gruff voice called. I turned to see the man with bulging muscles. In one hand he held a pistol, aimed right at my chest. "Put your hands up!"

My heart thundered against my ribs as I raised my hands in the air. The log book was clearly visible in one. I steeled myself to face the man and not glance over to where Paw stood in the shadows. He might be my only hope.

The man took a step toward me. Then another...

Paw lunged at the man's arm, clamping his jaws around his wrist and knocking him to the deck. The gun dropped from the man's hand and I dived for it. Paw released the guy and stood guarding him.

With the gun trained on the man, I called Paw to me. He trotted over to my side, proudly waving his tail.

I glanced down at Paw. "Good dog."

I bent over and picked up the log book with my free hand and carefully backed toward the stairs.

"Stay where you are while we –"

A voice came from my right. "Put down the gun."

My heart fell.

Paw growled low in his throat.

I turned. Jack was standing a few feet away holding a shotgun.

He hefted the shotgun and I sighed, placing my gun on the deck.

His voice hardened. "That mutt moves and I blast him between the eyes. Got it?

I grasped Paw's collar and pulled him protectively close to me. "Got it."

The captain came to stand alongside Jack. "What are you goin' to do with her? Lock her up like the other one?"

"No." Jack replied with a wicked grin. "No. I'm going to tie her and the mutt up and throw them overboard."

The captain nodded as he spoke to me. "Toss the book over here."

Suddenly the scene burst with light. Police boats and helicopters were everywhere. The captain rushed at me, trying to grab the log book. I kicked him in the stomach and hit him over the head with the book. Jack raced for the boat but didn't make it. With one flying leap Paw tackled him to the deck and growled into his face.

Police swarmed onto the boat. Within minutes, the rest of the crew were apprehended.

Paw and I were escorted onto one of the police boats.

A young officer offered me a blanket to wrap around my shoulders, asking, "Are you all right?"

I gave Paw a hug. "I am, thanks to my hero."

Paw licked my chin.

I looked back toward shore. "I have an idea where Carol might be."

A short boat ride, a short walk, and we were where I hoped to find Jac's Aunt Carol.

The movie theater.

Mounted on the roof of the gray cement building was a spotlight. Several grimy windows, some with broken panes, fronted the building. Weeds grew through the cement in the drive-in lot, competing with empty popcorn containers and soda cups.

Sergeant Gray shook his head. "You sure about this?"

I nodded. "It's my best guess. I saw the signal for the boat come from the movie theater tonight. Since Carol wasn't on the boat, this is the most obvious place."

The sergeant still looked doubtful, but ordered his men to search the place. Sergeant Gray commanded me to stay outside with Paw. He walked forward a few feet to watch.

Paw woofed in greeting. I turned to find Jac and Shelbee running toward me. They reached my side and we embraced in a group hug.

Jac pushed hair out of her eyes. "What's happening –"

A shout went up at the entrance to the theater. "Sarge, we found her."

My heart leapt into my throat. *Please let her be alive.*

Jac grabbed my hand in a viselike grip. "Is she –"

From the entrance, two officers escorted a woman wrapped in a blanket. Her hair was limp and she stumbled as she walked, but her eyes were alert.

Jac dropped my hand, running to the woman. "Aunt Carol!"

Carol pushed away from the officers and stumbled to Jac. "Jac! Is it really you?" They met and embraced, laughing and crying.

A Dog Detective Short Story Collection

Paw woofed excitedly.

Sergeant Gray placed a hand on my shoulder. "Take her home. She's been through a trial. I'll stop by in a few hours to take statements."

I smiled, grateful for his kindness.

We all went back to the house to comfort Aunt Carol. A warm bath, hot meal, and Aunt Carol was feeling better.

Jac sat down next to her aunt on the couch. "What happened to you, Aunt Carol?"

Carol sighed. "Let's wait until Sergeant Gray arrives. I'm too tired to tell it twice."

Paw curled up in front of the fireplace and I sat next to him rubbing his massive head.

Shelbee joined Jac and Carol on the couch.

Sergeant Gray arrived shortly, escorting Mr. Phillips in handcuffs.

Jac invited the men inside. Sergeant Gray pushed Mr. Phillips into one the couch's matching chairs then took the other for himself.

I shook my head in confusion. "Why is Mr. Phillips in handcuffs?"

Sergeant Gray took out his notebook and pen. "I'll explain that in a few minutes. First I want to take Aunt Carol's statement."

Aunt Carol nodded. "I have been investigating smuggling activity in the area. The wildlife in the area, particularly the sea life, has been dying. Fish have washed up on shore, etc. I went to the police with my concerns, but never saw any active investigation from them." She looked pointedly at the sergeant.

Gray blushed.

Aunt Carol sighed, "I continued to investigate on my own. I discovered the smuggling ring one night when I was searching the beach for dead fish. I took photos and began to track the smuggler's movements. Again, I went to the police who failed to act, in my opinion.

"I was frustrated so I decided to take matters into my own hands. Last Thursday, when I saw the signal, I decided to confront the smugglers –"

Jac gasped. "Aunt you could have been hurt."

Carol patted her hand. "I know that now. But I was so aggravated, I didn't think. I confronted the one they call Jack that night on the beach. As I was arguing with him, one of his men grabbed me from behind. Jack threw a sack over my head and tied my hands behind my back. They pushed me, stumbling, to walk."

Carol shuddered. "I didn't know where we were going." Tears dripped down her cheeks. "I thought they were going to kill me."

Mr. Phillips groaned and hung his head.

Jac handed her aunt a tissue. Wiping her eyes, Carol continued. "Sounds from the ocean had receded, so I knew we were heading inland. I heard the creak of a door opening and could smell mold. I was forced to walk down some rickety steps. They shoved me onto the floor and tied my feet together, then removed the sack and gagged me. I was so relieved when I heard them walk away and heard a door close overhead."

Jac hugged her aunt. Carol eased her grip on the tissue. "I struggled in vain for hours to loosen the ropes around my wrists, but the bindings were too tight.

"Eventually, Jack came back. I recognized his voice. He removed the gag and gave me a drink of water from a bottle. Then gagged me again. He repeated this at irregular intervals. He kept demanding to know where my evidence was hidden, but I refused to tell him."

Sergeant Gray closed his notebook.

Mr. Phillips shifted in his chair. "Carol, I must apologize for my son's behavior. I am appalled at his treatment of you. I had no idea he would act that way. I knew he was involved in the smuggling. That's why I tried to persuade you to stop investigating, but I didn't know he was the leader."

Still confused I asked Sergeant Gray, "How did the police get to the boat so quickly?"

Jac replied. "I can answer that. Shelb and I decided not to see the movie. We turned around and headed home. Mr. Phillips met us at the door. He said he knew what was going on and wanted to help. Paw was throwing a fit so I let him out. Then we saw your note and rushed to the police station."

Mr. Phillips said, "I want to apologize to you, too, Ms. Hayes."

He paused, studying the handcuffs. "When I found out Carol had disappeared, I knew I had to put a stop to the smuggling. My son was the one who sent the return signal.

He worked at the theater and ran the spotlight every Tuesday and Thursday. He also picked up the shipment."

He shook his head. "I am very sorry he tried to kill you, Ms. Hayes. I never thought Jack would get this out of control."

"Apology accepted, Mr. Phillips," I replied. "I had a feeling Jack was your son. He had the same cultured voice."

Sergeant Gray stood. He grasped Mr. Phillips by the arm, pulling him up from the chair.

Carol walked over and gave Mr. Phillips a kiss. She whispered. "You are forgiven."

Shelbee asked, "What will happen to the smugglers, Jack, and Mr. Phillips?"

Sergeant Gray slipped his notebook in his pocket. "The smugglers and Jack will go to prison for illegal contraband and kidnapping. Mr. Phillips will get a reduced sentence for his cooperation."

I yawned.

Exhausted, we all turned in for some well-deserved sleep.

The rest of the vacation went well. Jac took over running the movie theater and Shelbee went out with her lifeguard. Aunt Carol headed up the committee to clean up the beach and ocean.

As for me, I wrote a prize winning article on the smuggling and took it easy. Paw never scratched again and loved to go swimming.

I asked him, "Were you really finicky about water or were you trying to tell me something?" In reply he rolled his eyes, wagged his tail, and ran outside. I began to wonder what new adventure he would find for us.

A few moments later, Paw returned wearing a mischievous grin.

The aroma was staggering.

I groaned. "Oh, Pew! Paw, you stink! Don't tell me you rolled in dead fish *again*."

He just looked at me with those big, innocent eyes.

I knelt and embraced him, stink and all, in a huge hug. "It doesn't matter, Paw. You are the best dog a woman could ever have. Come on, we'll give you another bath." I sniffed my clothes. "And a shower for me. Then we'll go for a walk."

Paw leaned into my embrace, filling my heart with love.

3

THE MYSTERY OF THE BODY IN THE SHED

1990s

Snowflakes descended dancing a slow ballet to themselves. Some landed on my window creating a crystallized effect that turned the midmorning light into a kaleidoscope of colors. Others joined their fellow flakes on the ground which was completely covered in nearly three feet of snow. It looked as though a gigantic snowflake reunion had taken place. Grandparents and parents were communing with third cousins and even more distant relatives. Indeed, it was a beautiful sight.

If you didn't have to go out in it, that is. So far there had been no accidents in front of my house this morning. "My" meaning me, Clarissa Montgomery Hayes. Although I'm in my twenties, I look young to many people. I stand five-foot-two and have blonde hair and hazel eyes. Once people meet me, though, they find I'm mature and intelligent. I live on Main Street in a red brick, two-story house with white trim. I share it with my pet St. Bernard, Paudius Pernivious, nicknamed Paw. He came to me as a puppy with big brown eyes and a sweetly innocent expression. Little did I know he would grow to declare himself King Paw, ruler of his home and his master. I love him dearly.

Anyway, as I said, there hadn't been an accident this morning. For the past three days, accidents had become an everyday occurrence. Outside, the snow had covered everything in sight. To add to this nightmare, sleet fell every night covering the landscape with a "one step can kill ya" slippery sheen. Therefore, Paw and I had stayed indoors. Paw stretched before a blazing fire and I worked at my writing desk. I am a freelance writer and it being a week before Christmas, I had been assigned to write an article on Halloween. That may seem odd, but magazines worked on forward-looking deadlines. Which made it hard to think of pumpkins and black cats when surrounded by snow and sparkling Christmas lights. Sitting at my desk, pen in hand, I was contemplating what I'd write as I stared at the Christmas tree. That was when the phone rang.

Paw jumped up, grabbed the receiver with his mouth, and dropped it at my feet. This had become his favorite new trick for the last two days. A woman's voice on the line was desperately saying, "Hello, is anyone there? Hello? Hello?!"

"Yes, Hello," I politely replied. "I'm sorry about that."

"Oh, Clarissa, it is you. Thank God! I was afraid the

phone had gone dead." The voice trembled. "This is Mrs. Carstairs. Can you help me?"

I frowned – she sounded upset. I strove to keep my voice calm. "Mrs. Carstairs, I would be glad to help you if you could tell me what is wrong."

A stifled sob emerged from the phone. "What's wrong? Yes, of course. The door to the shed keeps banging. I want it closed. I can't go out to do it. Clarissa, I'm scared. Jason locked that door tight before the storm. I'm afraid there might be burglars here."

"It's ok, Mrs. Carstairs; Paw and I will be right over."

Mrs. Carstairs lived two blocks away in a beautiful old house built in 1901. She was a vibrant, generous soul who lived alone, even though she was 89 and arthritic. In the winter she seldom left her house except to go to church. But in this terrible weather she had spent the last two Sundays at home with only her grandson, Jason, visiting.

Paw and I started out on the sidewalk, but it remained too slippery. So we began walking in the snow which was no easy job. The sleet crust was too soft to walk on top but also hard to break through. The snow lay so high that my leg would sink in up to my thigh. Paw loved the snow and lunged forward eager to play. That made it even tougher on me as I tried to hold onto his leash and "walk" through the snow. Finally, after a half hour we reached Mrs. Carstairs' house.

Gingerly we stepped onto the front porch, which was covered with a heavy layer of ice and rang the doorbell. Mrs. Carstairs, a tiny, frail woman with gray hair and light blue eyes, opened the door cautiously and suspiciously peered at Paw and me. She then glanced from side to side and behind us. Finally, she beckoned us inside. Once we were in she locked the door. Mrs. Carstairs was definitely not herself. She would usually greet everyone with a hearty "Merry Christmas" and a plate of peanut butter cookies. I believe Paw would do anything for those cookies.

"I...I...I'm sorry to bother you," she uttered, half in a trance. She stood wringing her hands, continually darting glances in all directions.

"That's ok, Mrs. Carstairs. You wanted me to check the shed and lock the door. Right?" By now Paw knew there was something wrong. He had his ears alert, ready for any problem.

"Yes," Mrs. Carstairs replied, her mind clearly elsewhere.

Soothingly, I suggested she make some hot cocoa. I left Paw to keep her company and to reassure her that she would be safe. Leaving through the kitchen door, I crunched across the snow to reach the shed. I aimed to check the door and find the problem. Sure enough, the lock hung open on the door. I reached up to lock it when I felt a sudden chill. It wasn't the wind; it was the chill of danger running up my spine.

Slowly, I unhooked the lock and opened the door.

I stepped inside – and drew in my breath in shock.

On the floor lay a dead man. He was dressed in a navy blue uniform with the letters AP in bold green print on his shirt. I guessed his age to be mid-fifties with thinning, mousy brown hair and a bulging midriff. He had been shot straight between the eyes.

Shutting the door, I set the lock in place taking care to leave it open.

I rushed into the house and dialed 911.

A woman's voice answered. "911, what's the emergency?"

Speaking more calmly than I felt, I said, "There's a dead man in my neighbor's shed."

"What is your address?"

I rattled it off to her.

I could hear the dispatcher tapping keys as the she entered the address. She informed me, "The police are on their way."

I carefully hung up the phone.

I turned to Mrs. Carstairs who was pale.

I reassured her. "Everything will be okay. The police are on their way."

She half-smiled and her lids fluttered.

I dove toward her as her knees buckled. She was easy to catch since she was so tiny.

I helped her to the sofa in the den.

I brought her some hot cocoa. She sipped it quietly for a minute.

Then she said, "That was funny what you said."

Believing she thought I was joking, I said, "I'm so sorry, Mrs. Carstairs, but it's true. There is a dead man in your shed."

"No. No. Not that. You said it'll be okay and the police

are on their way. It rhymed. I know I shouldn't laugh at a time like this, but it's the first thing that came to mind."

"Oh. Yeah, that is funny. I'm sorry, Mrs. Carstairs."

She gave a soft shrug, "Call me Emma, please."

"Ok," I agreed. "Emma, I'm sorry this had to happen, but the police will soon be here."

"What I can't understand is the fact that I know Jason locked that door." Emma sighed.

In the distance I could hear the police sirens wailing. I opened the front door to find two blue and white squad cars parked at an angle to the curb. I guess they didn't receive too many dead body calls. Two young men were hurrying up the front steps. Both looked to be in their early-twenties and eager. Rookies. An older man followed at a slow, steady pace. He was a veteran officer and I knew him well. I should have known my Uncle Harry would have come personally to check this out. Anything regarding my name was closely investigated by Harry, who was quite protective.

At the age of fifty-four, Harry had a full head of wavy brown hair graying at the sides, with a square set jaw that often sent criminals to confessing. His ample girth and tall stature often won him the role of Santa Claus at Christmas. No wonder these rookies were so nervous. First, a dead body and now Uncle Harry.

As Harry walked up the steps, each officer stood to either side of the porch allowing Harry to take full command.

My dear uncle had this habit of making even questions

sound like serious statements. "What'd you get yourself into this time, young lady?"

I put my hands on my hips. "Uncle Harry, I do not GET myself into things. I didn't place the body in Mrs. Carstairs's shed. I just simply found it."

"Harrumph," Harry growled. It was a kindly growl meant to say "the things these young'uns get me into." He loved it every time he got involved.

I politely asked, "So would you like to see the body or have some tea first?" The two rookies' eyes widened. I could tell they figured we were joking, but they still weren't one hundred percent sure. Uncle Harry had that effect on people.

"Just show me where the body is and we'll take everything from here. And you stay in; it's too cold and slippery for you outside." By the way, Uncle Harry was also the chief of police. He usually got things his way. I didn't argue, this time.

Passing by the living room, he waved to Mrs. Carstairs, saying, "Mornin', Emma." Paw came to greet Harry and got a friendly pat on the head. Then Harry and the officers stepped out the back door and proceeded to the shed.

Paw and I kept a silent vigil watching the shed. All three went inside. After five minutes, they emerged - the two rookies, having paled, and Harry not even fazed. He left the rookies to stand guard and trudged back to the house.

As he passed through the kitchen to the telephone in the hallway, he commented, "Some bloody business this is!" The statement was figurative not literal. There had been no blood; at least none that I saw. I stood listening to his conversation and mentally noting the important parts.

"...send the coroner ...get the forensics team over here pronto ...hold all my calls." Uncle Harry hung up the phone. I assumed he had been talking to his personal secretary, Miss May.

Harry turned and gave me orders. "Stay here. Direct the coroner and the rest of my men to the shed. Do not talk to reporters. I repeat DO NOT TALK TO REPORTERS. If the phone rings - don't answer it."

"You think reporters will be here already?"

"Yes, I do. I was at the diner when I got your message. Of course, Old Freddy was there. I'm sure he couldn't wait to tell the local newspapers and TV station." Uncle Harry's mouth turned down. Old Freddy was the biggest gossip in town. I had no doubt Harry was right.

I nodded assent and he returned to the shed. Within half an hour the coroner and the rest of the police arrived. Shortly thereafter the phone began to ring constantly, so I unplugged it. Once, I opened the door and camera flash bulbs nearly blinded me. Reporters were yelling questions in order to be heard. I closed and locked the door and didn't open it from then on.

By late afternoon the police had finished. The body was at the coroner's office. The shed, thoroughly photographed, dusted for prints, and otherwise investigated, was now locked and the door sealed with "Police...Do Not Disturb" tape. Uncle Harry had made a statement to the reporters and dispersed them to their newspaper and TV homes.

Uncle Harry was the last to leave. As he stood with me and Mrs. Carstairs in the kitchen, he warned me, "From now on try to stay out of trouble, please! And be careful. The killer may still be out there."

My brow creased. "So you are writing it up as a homicide?"

"Yes. So watch your back. Watch Emma, too. It could be whoever killed him may come back. He may think you know something."

He looked between us with a worried frown. "You don't, do you?"

I shook my head. "No. I've told you everything."

Emma also shook her head. "I had no idea he was out there. Do you think they were burglars and one of them turned on the other?"

Harry's brows creased. "I thought you told the officers that nothing was stolen?"

Emma shivered. "No, but maybe they turned on each other before they got to stage the heist. You see that all the time on those new cop shows."

He sighed with a shake of his head. "Emma, I've told you to stop watching those shows. I have no knowledge of any burglaries in town recently. Those shows only worry you."

"You can learn a lot from those shows, Harry." She sniffed and walked into the kitchen.

Harry looked at me with resignation. "That woman is going to drive me crazy."

I walked him to the front door.

"Thanks for the concern." I hugged Harry goodbye.

"I'm stationing a uniformed patrol car out front. He'll be here in a few minutes."

A moment later he left in his squad car.

Returning to the kitchen, I found Mrs. Carstairs mixing flour and eggs in a bowl. Why? I wondered. As if she knew my thoughts she responded, "Baking cookies helps me to relax." She wiped her hands and walked over to me. Hesitantly, she asked, "Clarissa, would you mind spending a night or two here? Jason went home this morning. After today I feel rather lonely in this house by myself."

I smiled. "Sure. I would be happy to. I'll just go to my house and get a few things. Paw can stay here."

"That's all right. Take Paw with you. I'll have dinner ready when you return." She went back to her cookies.

Paw and I trudged home through lightly falling snow. I packed a suitcase with clothes and put Paw's things in a cardboard box. Also, I grabbed my writing supplies to finish the story for my editor.

When I went to close the drapes in the living room, I received quite a shock. A white car had pulled into my driveway. I remembered seeing it parked in front of Mrs. Carstairs's when I left.

The doorbell rang. I briefly caught a glimpse of a dark-haired man in a blue winter coat. Taking Paw by the collar, I went to answer the door.

"Hello," I said flatly, "can I help you?"

"Hello, you're Miss Hayes, right? The chief told me to watch over you. I just wanted to let you know I'm here." He stood six feet with broad shoulders and had warm brown eyes.

I looked him over with suspicion. "How do I know the chief sent you?" He didn't look like a police officer to me. I could feel Paw shift his weight getting into a stance for lunging. He didn't trust this guy either.

He smiled gently. "Uncle Harry told me to call you Gingersnap. He said you'd know what that means."

"Because I used to love gingersnap cookies," I said. It was a test. The truth is I never liked gingersnaps.

He smiled. "Well, no. From his story you hated gingersnap cookies and he loved them." He was young, in his mid-twenties, with an air of confidence.

"Yes. That is correct. Sorry about the grilling, but Harry told me to watch my back." I smiled, letting him in the house.

"I was worried when you left. I came to check on you. My name is Bruce Severs." We shook hands.

"Call me Clarissa. I came to get some things since I will be staying with Mrs. Carstairs. By the way, you don't look much like a policeman." I snapped on Paw's leash and continued gathering my suitcase, box, and writing supplies.

"Here, let me take that." He took the suitcase and box. "It's started to snow. I'll drive you over there." He headed for the car. I locked up and Paw and I got in. "Oh, and I'm not a cop. I'm a private detective. Your uncle sometimes asks me to do favors for him. This is one."

The rest of the trip we mostly talked about Harry. When we arrived at Emma's house, the patrol car was parked outside. Bruce helped me carry my things to the door. I asked him inside, but he refused. Bruce was determined to stand guard.

Paw and I entered the house and I could smell a delicious meal cooking. I unpacked and went downstairs for dinner. Paw ate his meal in two seconds flat. Did I say ate? I should have said inhaled. Before long he wanted to go out. I opened the back door and let him go about his business. While waiting on him, I helped clear the table.

I looked around the kitchen. "Let me help you with the dishes, Emma?"

"No, dear. I'll take care of them. I'm just glad to have you here. You go upstairs and relax."

"Thank you. I do have my article to finish." I opened the back door and Paw sauntered in, dropping a shiny object at my feet. I picked it up.

Emma turned with interest. "What's that, dear?"

"It's a gold cigarette lighter," I said, trying to light it. "It doesn't work, though. Probably lay in the cold too long." I turned it over. There were black initials in bold print: CG.

Emma shrugged. "Probably one of the policemen dropped it."

"Maybe." The lighter looked too expensive for a cop. I pocketed it to look at later. Right now I had to "de-snow" Paw. His legs were caked with snow and ice that was melting all over the kitchen.

After cleaning up Paw and the kitchen, I went upstairs. I sat down and finished my article on Halloween. I titled it - "Black Cats or Bats". Not the most original, but I had tried to give it a different angle. Before going to bed I looked out the window. Bruce's white car was gone, but the patrol car was still there. It was time to get some sleep.

I awoke early to find Paw curled up in bed with me. Paw didn't like new places and often reacted this way. Deciding to make breakfast for Mrs. Carstairs, I got dressed. Before I left the room I did two things. First, I checked to see if the patrol car was out front. It was, but I didn't see Bruce's car.

Next, I informed Paw he could stay here or come with me for breakfast. He gave me a look that said "You gotta be kidding!" and nestled into the blankets.

"Fine," I replied. "I'll leave the door open if you change your mind." He ignored me.

However, by the time I reached the stairs, he was right behind me. His stomach had won out. When we reached the kitchen, I found Mrs. Carstairs up and preparing breakfast.

"Good mornin', dear." Her voice rang with cheer. "I hope you like scrambled eggs and bacon."

"Sounds delicious. I'll set the table." Smiling, I gathered the plates.

The phone rang and Emma went to answer it. I heard some murmuring and then she burst into tears. I switched off the stove and ran to be by her side. She hung up the phone and turned to me, tears streaming down her face.

"The police have arrested Jason. How could that be? He'd never hurt a fly!"

I stared in astonishment. "Why?"

"He...was the last...person... to lock the shed."

She sagged.

I embraced her and helped her over to the couch.

I held Emma while she cried.

After a few minutes, Emma wiped at her tears and pulled from my embrace. Her face steeled with determination. "I've gotta go see him. I'll sort this out."

I stood up. "All right. I'll go and speak to the patrol officer out front. You bundle up, Emma. It's cold out."

I put on my coat.

Paw hurried to the door ahead of me.

I grabbed his collar. "Sorry, boy. You have to stay here. Guard the house."

He woofed and sat down.

I stepped outside and walked to the patrol car.

The officer rolled down his window at my approach. "Problem?"

I smiled. "Mrs. Carstairs wants to go to the police station. Can you take us?"

He nodded. "Sure thing."

Emma stepped out of the house and I hurried to her side to assist her.

The officer jumped out of his car and offered Emma his arm. She smiled at him as he helped her into the back of the car.

I sat in back with Emma.

Once at the station, Emma went to see Jason and I found Harry.

Harry shook his head. "I know what you're going to say, but I had no choice. His fingerprints were found at the scene. And," he stopped me from interrupting, "his prints

A Dog Detective Short Story Collection

were on the guy's comb in his pocket."

"How did you match his prints? Don't they have to be on file?" I was confused.

"His prints were on file. A few years ago he worked at a company that had a rash of thefts. The employees were asked to voluntarily have their fingerprints taken to rule them out. Jason volunteered."

"Can he explain the prints on the comb?"

"No. He says he has no idea how they got there. And no, before you ask, I haven't got an ID on the victim. I looked up the companies with the logo AP, but none had ever heard of the guy." He paused and then said, "Clarissa, I want you to stay out of this."

"Harry, you know I can't!"

He grimaced. I knew that look. It meant he would persist until I gave in so I turned and left his office. I went to sit in the front lobby to wait for Mrs. Carstairs.

At last Mrs. Carstairs came out from her visit, looking pale and shaken. I had the officer take us all home. She remained subdued.

At home she sighed. "I'm going to take a nap. I need some quiet time, dear."

Sensing she wanted to be alone I decided to visit my editor. The article was due and I needed to get out and clear my mind. I walked Paw back to our house, checked the mail, and then got us into our car. I noticed Bruce was back on the job. His white car followed us.

I dropped my article at my editor's office and decided to take the scenic route home. I had no intentions of losing

Bruce, but it would give him something to do. The road took us through the high-class part of town. This was where the rich lived in expensive houses, grocery stores offered caviar, and business prices tripled. I was admiring the scraped clean pavement and sidewalks when suddenly Paw began barking and waving his tail. I had to pull off the road to stop the face slashing I was getting from his tail.

"Paw! Calm down!" I shouted. He continued to bark and paw at the window.

"Paw! Stop that!"

"Woof! Woof!" He turned, looking at me as though to say I was stupid. Then he looked out the window again. "Woof!"

By now I realized my intelligent dog was trying to tell me something. I looked out the window, my mouth dropping open. There across the parking lot was a fitness club for the rich. Atop the white brick structure stood the bold green letters AP, signifying the Altogether Perfect fitness club's name. Harry hadn't considered them. For one thing they were an exclusive club for the wealthy. You had to be "somebody" to get in. Furthermore, they weren't listed in the phone book or on any advertisements. They didn't need to be.

"Good boy!" I told Paw. He now settled down. He'd got his point across.

I wished I had one of those new cellphones that were becoming popular. Instead, I drove back to Emma's and called Harry.

"Uncle, I found a new clue regarding the body I found -"

He growled. "I told you to stay out of it. This is police work."

I argued, "But Uncle, you know I can help. I've solved mysteries in the past -"

He raised his voice. "Minor incidents, Clarissa. This is serious. A killer is on the loose. Now stay in the house with Emma and mind your own business."

Click.

My jaw dropped.

He had hung up on me.

Paw nudged my hand with his big, wet nose.

Fine. Since Uncle Harry didn't want my help, then I'd investigate on my own.

"Let's say we visit that club tonight, ok?"

Paw wagged his tail with delight.

Now all I had to do was figure how to elude my "bodyguard" and how to get into the club. Neither was going to be easy. I began to formulate a plan. The only problem was how to avoid Bruce.

Emma came downstairs. "I thought I heard you talking."

I put my arm around her. "Come into the living room. I want to talk to you."

She put a hand to her throat. "Is something wrong? Is it Jason?"

I smiled. "No, but I have a plan to help him."

We settled on the couch. Paw stretched out at my feet.

I told her about the club I found. "I want to search that club for evidence, but I need help."

Emma shook her head. "It's too dangerous. Talk to Harry again. I know he'll listen."

I scowled. "Uncle is convinced Jason is guilty. He won't listen."

She frowned in thought. Reluctantly, she nodded her head. "What do you need me to do?"

"Your granddaughter, Sarah, is about my size. Can you get her to visit this evening?""

Emma's eyes widened. "How will that help?"

I smiled. "If Sarah's willing, I can dress in her clothes and take her car. Bruce won't realize it's me so he won't follow."

Emma went to call her granddaughter.

Sarah agreed to help.

I drove home to get the supplies I needed and returned to Emma's. Bruce followed the whole time.

Sarah was there when I got back.

I changed into Sarah's clothes. We were roughly the same height and build. With her clothes, some make-up, and her car, I hoped to elude Bruce.

In Sarah's clothes, with a handbag of essentials, Paw and I walked to her car. We got in, started up, and drove away. After driving three blocks, I felt sure Bruce hadn't followed. Then I turned onto a side street and drove to the fitness club.

In the parking lot I changed clothes. I hoped to convince the management that I was a police security consultant. Since I had spent many years around Uncle Harry and the police squad, I knew their dress and actions. Paw and I then entered the fitness club.

A receptionist greeted us with concern. "I'm sorry, but there are no dogs allowed."

I kept my tone curt, simulating the mannerisms of an overworked security consultant. "This is a certified security dog; his nose is one of the finest in the states." I wrapped my hand around his leash. "Didn't you get the memo from corporate? We're doing a sweep for drugs this afternoon. Part of our zero-tolerance policy."

"Oh," she replied hesitantly. "Wait here. I'll get the manager."

The manager soon arrived. He was in his mid-thirties with slick black hair and a smooth manner, wearing a tailored suit.

His smile was a little too wide. "How may I help you?"

I replied flatly, "I'm here for the security sweep. It should be quick; we haven't had any trouble at any of the other branches."

Paw's eyes never left his face.

The manager's lips stayed in a smile, but his eyes darted from side to side. "Do you have some ID?"

I showed him my ID. Basically, it was a fake badge, but the ID card was real. It had been a joke gift from one of Harry's police friends. I found it came in quite handy. Apparently, the manager was satisfied.

"My name is Kid Garcon." He waved a hand toward the stairs. "I'd be happy to show you around."

I shrugged. "Up to you, if you want to waste your time."

His hand strayed to his shirt pocket where I could see a pack of cigarettes, but then his eyes flicked to the large "No

Smoking" sign on the wall. He licked his lips nervously. "We haven't had any problems with drugs here, I can tell you."

We entered the fitness room. State of the art equipment filled the room where tanned and toned men and women wore workout outfits that cost more than my car. A few people glanced curiously at Paw, but most stared avidly at the overhead TVs scrolling stock market updates.

Mr. Garcon watched Paw nervously. "Is he sensing anything?"

I glanced at Paw. His stance was relaxed as he sniffed the air.

I shook my head. "Let's proceed to the staff break room."

We returned to the hallway.

The manager took me to a door at the end of the hallway. "This is the break room. I -"

An overhead speaker chimed. "Mr. Garcon. Please come to reception."

Garcon frowned. "I'll be right back."

I waved him off. "We'll continue our security scan."

He hesitated, but then scurried away.

Paw and I opened the door to the break room and stepped inside. No employees were around. I closed the door.

There were a row of five lockers along the wall. I opened the first one. A dark blue parka hung on the peg. I felt the pockets, but they were empty. A muddy pair of boots sat on the locker floor.

I closed the locker and checked the next one. It was

locked. Leaving it, I tried the third locker. It opened smoothly; however, it was empty.

I closed the door and looked over to where Paw was sniffing under the break room table.

I turned to the fourth locker and lifted the latch. It stuck so I jiggled it, opening it with a soft pop.

Paw looked up. I hoped the sound didn't attract attention.

Sweat was starting to trickle down my back.

I searched the locker. It contained a paper bag on the top shelf. Inside was a blackened banana. Hanging on the peg was a navy blue uniform with a green AP logo on the front of the shirt, just like the dead man wore. I patted the pockets - empty.

A small snow shovel was wedged into a corner of the locker.

I heard voices in the hallway. I wiped my brow with my sleeve and closed the locker door.

Hurrying, I tried the last locker. This one was locked, too.

The voices faded as whoever was in the hall walked away.

I picked up Paw's leash, opened the break room door, and peered out.

The hallway was empty.

I decided that now would be a good time to search the manager's office. Hopefully, he was still detained at reception.

Paw and I moved down the hallway, passing a door marked "Closet."

Paw stopped and sniffed the crack of the door. He turned his head and stared at me.

I opened the closet and peered inside.

Ten of the navy blue uniforms with the bold green initials AP on the shirt were hanging in the closet.

We needed to find more proof before I spoke to Uncle Harry.

I closed the closet door and we found the manager's office.

I entered his office without knocking. Obviously, I surprised him for he jumped up out of his chair.

"I'm sorry, I didn't realize you were here."

The office was large, appointed with expensive mahogany furniture, and from the smell, apparently a new carpet had been put in.

Paw found one section interesting and began to dig at the carpeting.

"Stop that!" I commanded. Grabbing his collar, I simply said to Mr. Garcon, "Sorry".

I was positive I knew what Paw had found. That, along with the ashtray of cigarette butts on the manager's desk, confirmed my suspicion of his guilt. Now all I had to do was get out and hope Harry could help. Shaking Mr. Garcon's hand, I indicated Paw, "He has found no trace of drug activity in your building. I will state that in my report. Thank you for your time."

Paw growled menacingly.

I spun around.

Bruce, the private detective Uncle Harry had sent to watch me, stood in the doorway with his hands raised.

Behind him was a large man with a scar running across his left eye. He marched Bruce into the room at gunpoint.

Scar-eye pointed at me. "Hey, I know her. Kid, she's the one who found Louis's body.

Garcon came around his desk. "I knew it! There's no way you were a security consultant. Not with that mutt."

I replied, "He's smarter than you are. He knew you were a criminal."

Scar-eye asked, "What do you want me to do with them?"

Kid said, "Tie them up and -"

I had one chance to save us. I unhooked Paw's leash. "Paw. Go!"

Paw leaped away from me.

As Scar-eye lunged for Paw, who easily evaded him, Bruce twisted and brought up his leg, kicking Scar-eye in the chest.

Scar-eye dropped the gun.

Someone grabbed me. The voice said, "Don't move."

I cursed. I had been so distracted by Paw and Bruce that I failed to pay attention to Garcon.

He pulled me tight against him, pressing a gun to my head. "You," he nodded to Bruce, "Back off."

Bruce moved away from Scar-eye who struggled to his feet and retrieved his gun.

Garcon laughed. "Your mutt wasn't so loyal after all. He's

run off." He motioned to his accomplice. "Let's lock them up."

A minute later and we were trussed up in the dark closet with the company uniforms. As they walked away, Garcon muttered something about a mangy mutt. Hope rose. As long as Paw was free, we stood a chance.

Bruce and I struggled at our bonds, but they had been tied tightly.

Bruce said, "Don't worry. We'll get out of this."

I heard scratching outside the door.

"I'm not worried. I have a Paw."

"What's a –"

The handle to the door rattled.

Bruce snorted. "You mean the dog. He can't-"

Slowly the handle turned down.

The door popped open and Paw sauntered in.

"Good boy. Now help me get out of these ropes."

Paw chewed through the ropes, gentling his bite against my skin. In a moment, my hands were free.

I made quick work of untying the ropes around my feet, then untied Bruce.

He shook his head in admiration. "That's one great dog." He patted Paw on the head.

Paw beamed, waving his tail proudly.

Bruce took my hand. "Now, let's get out of here."

He took the lead, carefully peering around the door to make sure the coast was clear before leading us down the hallway. Paw stayed loyally by my side.

The reception area was empty and the entry doors were right in front of us –

A voice behind us said, "Hold it!"

We turned.

Scar-eye was standing by the desk, his pistol aimed square at my chest. Garcon was at his side.

Garcon shook his head. "Just shoot them. I'll make up a story later."

Scar-eye's good eye narrowed -

Bruce flew into motion, his body a blur. He tackled Scar-eye; the pistol went flying into the air. The two tumbled to the ground.

Garcon burst into flight, heading back down the hallway, Paw in hot pursuit.

I grabbed up the phone. My fingers hit 9-1-1.

By the time Harry arrived, Garcon and his accomplice were tied up with Paw standing guard.

Harry scolded me, "From now on you stay out of trouble, young lady."

"You're right, Uncle," I said and gave him a kiss.

Harry held out his hand to Bruce. "Thank you for your help."

Bruce shook his hand. "You're welcome, but Clarissa and Paw are the ones who found the criminals.

A cop escorted Garcon by us as Scar-eye was struggling to break from his guards.

Harry held up a hand to stop them. He stepped in front of Garcon. "You got anything to say?"

Garcon straightened his shoulders. "I am innocent." He gestured to Scar-eye. "He's the one who killed Louis."

Scar-eye yelled, "Oh, no, you don't. You're not putting the blame on me."

Garcon growled, "Shut up!"

Harry smirked. "How'd you know the dead man was named Louis?"

Garcon smirked back. "It was in the paper."

I piped up. "No, it wasn't." Garcon's smile faded

Harry scowled at me.

He turned back to Garcon. "Whoever tells me the truth has a better chance with the judge."

Garcon and Scar-eye spoke over each other.

Harry held up his hand. "Enough! Garcon, you go first." Harry glared at Scar-eye to be quiet.

Garcon swallowed nervously. "I killed Louis. He was blackmailing me."

Scar-eye interjected, "If you'd kept your pants on, he wouldn't have blackmailed you."

Bruce leaned on the check-in desk. "What's he mean by that?"

Garcon huffed. "It's personal."

Scar-eye laughed nastily. "Nothing personal about messing around with the boss's wife."

Garcon glowered at Scar-eye. "I ordered Fat Henry," he motioned to Scar-eye, "to get rid of the body. We put him in the car and dumped him at that mechanic's house where the old lady lives, out in the shed."

Harry narrowed his eyes. "Why there?"

Scar-eye smiled. "I saw that mechanic talkin' to Louis out front. Figured they were friends. I knew Louis was blackmailing Kid so I followed the mechanic to see where he lived. Thought he might be in on the blackmail."

Harry humphed. He waved the cops away. "Take them down to the station."

Then he turned to me. "Show me these clues you endangered yourself to find."

I took him to the closet and showed him the uniforms. Harry just grunted. Then I took him to Garcon's office.

I pointed to the cigarette butts in the ashtray on the desk. "Garcon has a smoking habit. Paw found a gold lighter in the snow at Emma's."

Harry exploded. "You found evidence and didn't report it?"

I glared at him. "Uncle, it was after the lab guys were gone. I let Paw out and he came back with it. I didn't know it was evidence and still don't for sure." I motioned around the room at the furniture. "But based on Garcon's office and clothes, it appears to me he has expensive taste. A gold lighter fits with his image."

Bruce asked, "Where is the lighter now?"

I smiled. "At Emma's."

Bruce said, "Easy enough to retrieve."

Harry nodded reluctantly. "Anything else?"

I nodded and pointed to the carpet. "It's brand new."

Paw was scratching at the same spot again.

I smiled. "You'll want the lab boys to look at that."

Harry hunched down and pulled at the edge of the

carpet. Bruce helped him roll it up. They revealed a large red stain on the floor underneath.

Blood stains.

Harry called in the lab guys and radioed for one of his men to pick up the cigarette lighter from Emma's.

Harry left his sergeant in charge. He pointed to me. "We're going back to the station. You and Paw ride with Bruce."

"Uncle-"

He waved me toward Bruce's car. "I'll send an officer to return Sarah's car."

As we got in Bruce's car, I asked him, "All right, mister. How did you know I was going here?"

He laughed. "That was easy. I followed you."

"But I never saw you. Besides, how did you know it was me?"

He smiled mischievously. "I know your walk and I doubted Paw would go with anybody else. I just waited and then followed you at a longer distance."

I never considered Paw when I had planned my disguise. I just automatically assumed he would go where I went, I suppose.

We, and Harry, arrived at the station right behind the officer who had stopped at Emma's. The officer held up an evidence bag with the lighter inside.

Harry took it to the interview room where Garcon was being held. Bruce, Paw and I followed. "This yours?"

Garcon nodded. "I spell my first name with a 'C'."

A Dog Detective Short Story Collection

Next all four of us moved to the other interview room, where Jason sat waiting.

Harry held up a photo of the dead man. "You sure you don't recognize this guy?"

Jason growled, "I told you I don't know him."

Harry nodded. "You a mechanic?"

"Yes."

"Ever go out for an emergency at the AP fitness club?"

Jason nodded thoughtfully. "Yes." His eyes widened. "Show me that photo again."

Harry held it up.

Jason smiled. "Now I remember the guy. His car wouldn't start. He was stuck in the parking lot of that fitness club." He thought some more. "Hey, wait a minute. Now I remember. The guy dropped his comb when he paid me. I picked it up for him." He laughed in relief. "That's how my prints got on the comb."

Harry nodded and the four of us left the room.

He handed the evidence and photo to one of his officers. "I'll call Emma."

He slapped Bruce on the back. "Take her home."

I kissed Harry. "Have a good evening."

He grunted.

Bruce walked Paw and me out to his car.

Once we were settled in the car with Paw in the backseat, Bruce asked me, "Would you like to go out to dinner?"

Paw woofed.

We both laughed.

I smiled at Bruce. "I would love to, but you'll have to include Paw in the invitation."

Bruce smiled. "No problem. There's a restaurant on Sweet Street that just opened. It caters to humans and dogs."

"The Whole Family Eats?" I asked, mentioning the restaurant Shelbee had told me about.

"That's the one."

"Excellent. I've been meaning to eat there."

A short drive and we were at the restaurant. Through the front picture windows, I could see people and dogs dining.

We entered, Paw greeting several dogs as we passed, and seated ourselves near the back of the restaurant.

Every dog in the place appeared happy and content.

Bruce held my chair to seat me, then slid into his own chair.

Paw sat at my feet.

A waitress in a blue uniform with a white apron placed menus and utensils in front of me and Bruce. "What can I get you folks to drink?"

Bruce pushed his menu to the side. "I'll take coffee."

I smiled at the waitress. "Tea, please. Herbal if you have it." I nodded to Paw. "And water for him."

The waitress nodded. "Be right back."

I leaned forward. "How long have you been a private detective?"

Bruce fidgeted with his fork. "Three years. I was on the police force, but decided to go out on my own. What about you? Is this your first case?"

I smiled. "No, not the first. I've solved a few other mysteries."

Paw woofed.

I laughed. "I mean we've solved a few."

The waitress arrived with our drinks order. "Let me know when you want to order."

We nodded.

Bruce picked up his cup. "A toast to solving mysteries. May we encounter many more, together."

I blushed and raised my cup. "To mysteries that we solve together."

Paw placed his head on my lap.

I scratched his ears. "Yes, Paw, to mysteries we all solve together."

Bruce saluted with his cup. "Hear, Hear."

4

THE MYSTERY OF THE MISSING BEAR

1990s

The late afternoon sun shone through the open French doors. Jac and Shelbee were serving Mrs. Booksteen tea. As Jac passed the plate of cookies she asked, "How was your trip to Hawaii, Mrs. Booksteen?"

"It was lovely, dear. They have the most beautiful flowers. I told Harold that we should have brought some back with us. But you know how my husband hates any extra baggage. He was sure it would cost too much. Oh, well, I suppose I have enough gardening to do as it is."

"You do grow the most beautiful flowers," I said as I accepted a cup of tea. "Your rhododendrons in the spring are always awash in color. I wish I had your green thumb."

"Clarissa, you are too modest. You are a good gardener.

With a little more experience you will be truly competent." Mrs. Booksteen smiled encouragingly.

Or was that condescendingly? I shook my head and said to myself, Clarissa Montgomery Hayes you need to be more understanding. Mrs. Booksteen's garden success may be the only bright spot in her life.

Mrs. Booksteen took a sip of her tea. "I was fortunate to have Mr. Reynolds, that's our next door neighbor, plant my newest rhododendron while I was gone. He said it was the least he could do because Harold took those books for him to Hawaii. I was furious at that nursery for making a delivery while we were away. I told them to wait until we were back. No one listens these days…." Mrs. Booksteen continued talking but I admit I stopped listening.

Thinking of her garden made me think of my Saint Bernard, Paw. Paw's full name is Paudius Pernivious, but I call him Paw since he loves to dig. I could only hope that he was behaving himself in Mrs. Booksteen's garden. Paw goes almost everywhere with me. I must admit that I have him horribly spoiled. Mrs. Booksteen's nephew, Arnold, was to be in the garden with Paw keeping him from mischief, especially digging in his aunt's garden. I had my doubts that he could accomplish this task. Paw can be devious and determined when he wants to do something. Arnold was an intelligent and capable boy at ten years old. It remained to be seen if Paw would outsmart him.

Suddenly something came hurtling through the French doors and landed with a plop in the middle of the tea tray on the coffee table. Dishes shattered, the teapot toppled over sending tea splashing everywhere, and cookies tumbled to the floor. We all froze, shocked by the sudden event. Then everyone started talking at once.

"What was that?" Jac said, looking bewildered.

"My tea service!" Mrs. Booksteen exclaimed.

"Is that a baseball?" Shelbee inquired.

"Where did it come from?" I asked.

"Arnold!" Mrs. Booksteen bellowed. "What did you do?" She jumped up from the sofa, a feat I didn't think possible, and charged out the French doors.

Shelbee, Jac, and I followed. I could only hope that Paw had nothing to do with this little incident. I stepped outside to see my furry friend lying in the grass behaving himself. Releasing a sigh of relief, I turned to see two boys, one of them Arnold, being interrogated by Mrs. Booksteen.

"I'm sorry, Aunt Alma. It was an accident. We were playing catch and I threw the ball too high for Billy to catch." Arnold looked remorseful.

"No, I should have caught it. I am so sorry, Mrs. Booksteen. It won't happen again. It's my fault that we were playing catch." The other boy, Billy I presumed, scuffed his toe in the dirt. He appeared to be several years younger than Arnold.

Mrs. Booksteen sighed. "You must be Billy Reynolds. You live next door, right?" The boy nodded. "Well, I suppose no real harm was done, but I can't let this go unpunished. The two of you will help me tomorrow afternoon in the garden. You can pull weeds to repay the damage to the tea set. Besides, someone could have been hurt by that ball. You need to learn to be accountable for your actions."

Both boys groaned at the mention of pulling weeds but nodded in agreement.

Billy said, "I will have to check with my mom if I can come over tomorrow."

"You most certainly can," said a stern voice behind us. Turning I saw a tall man step through the gap in the hedge between Mrs. Booksteen's yard and the one next door. "You will come over here tomorrow afternoon and help Mrs. Booksteen," the man affirmed.

"Mr. Reynolds." Mrs. Booksteen inclined her head to him.

"Mrs. Booksteen." He nodded. Looking at Billy he said, "Now get your things. We are going home."

Billy grimaced and began gathering his ball and glove. He looked around like he couldn't find something so I walked over to him.

"Are you missing something?" I asked.

He looked up at me and nodded. "My bear. I was sure I brought him over with me."

Mr. Reynolds glared. "Your bear. You mean you have lost your teddy bear. Billy, you are getting very irresponsible. Now find it this instant."

I would have liked to have given him a piece of my mind, but Mrs. Booksteen caught my eye and shook her head. Instead of saying anything, I began to hunt for the bear as did Jac, Shelbee, and Arnold. We looked all over the yard but found no bear.

Mr. Reynolds was getting visibly upset by the minute. Finally, he exploded, saying, "Billy, you better find that bear. Where were you before you came to Mrs. Booksteen's?"

Paw stood up and gave a low growl. I grabbed his collar just in case he chose to defend Billy. Paw is usually a gentle giant, but he doesn't let anyone harm or bully his friends.

Billy seemed to cringe. "I was playing ball against the toolshed."

"Fine. We will go back to our yard and search there. Let's go!" With that, Mr. Reynolds turned on his heel and stalked off. No thank yous, I'm sorrys, or goodbyes. Billy turned to follow him.

Mrs. Booksteen called after the boy. "Billy!" He turned. She continued, "You are always welcome to come over to my house to visit. Arnold will be visiting for the next two weeks. I am sure he would welcome the company." Arnold nodded his head in agreement.

Billy smiled weakly, "Thank you. I will be over tomorrow to help pull weeds." Then he turned and slipped through the hedge.

Mrs. Booksteen turned to Arnold. "Come, Arnold. You can help me clean up the mess in the living room." Arnold followed her into the house.

Jac, Shelbee, and I stood together staring next door. "I really don't like that man," Jac said.

"I feel sorry for Billy," Shelbee said.

"Yes, I agree with both of you." By now, Paw had come over for attention. I petted his head, thinking it had been odd that he had been so quiet up until now. He hadn't even joined in the search for the teddy bear. Shaking my head, I said, "Let's go help Mrs. Booksteen and then go home." Shelbee and Jac agreed and we went back inside. Mrs. Booksteen refused our help and we all went home.

The next day I decided to bake cookies for Arnold and Billy. I admit this was partly due to procrastination. I had a book I was working on and was suffering a mild case of writer's block. Baking cookies seemed a good way to avoid sitting down and writing. Of course, I had to bake some dog cookies for Paw too. Did I mention I had spoiled him?

The phone rang while I was mixing the cookie dough. It was Bruce Severs. Bruce had become a good friend. We had met when Mrs. Carstairs had her troubles. We now visited or talked nearly every day.

"How are you?" I asked.

"Busy." He sighed. "I'm going to be engrossed in this case for a while." Bruce was a private investigator. He spent a lot of time helping the police.

I teased him, "Am I allowed to know what you are working on or is it confidential?"

"All I can tell you is that it has to do with a string of pawnshop robberies. You probably read about the one in town in the newspaper. There have been others in the area."

"Anything in particular taken?"

"I can't tell you all of it, but the usual types of things: jewelry, watches, gold coins, plus some rare books and oddly enough, a painting. Listen I've got to go. I'll catch up with you soon and we will have dinner." Bruce waited for me to say goodbye and hung up. I missed his company when he was so busy. Jac and Shelbee had met him and continued to tease me about when we would become a couple. I would just tell them that they were being busybodies to which they would laugh.

The cookie baking was almost done. Paw had been determined to help me with baking his cookies and had somehow managed to get flour everywhere. I spent several minutes wiping down counters and mopping the floor while the last cookies baked. I was just finishing when the phone rang again.

Jac asked, "Hey, how about going shopping this afternoon?"

I sighed. "Well, I really should write."

"Yes, but you don't want to. Am I right?"

Laughing, I agreed. "So what are we shopping for? Anything in particular?"

"Dad's birthday is coming up," Jac said. "I want to get him a new wrench. You know he has been trying to repair the plumbing in the house. He wants to do it all himself, but he doesn't have up-to-date tools. His old wrench doesn't work right anymore, but he refuses to buy a new one. I figure if I get him a new one he'll use it and get done more quickly."

"Good plan. I love your dad, but he can be stubborn. I'll see you this afternoon." I hung up the phone and got the last batch of cookies out of the oven. I would have enough time to take them to Mrs. Booksteen's and then meet Jac. I would take Paw with me to Mrs. Booksteen's house since I couldn't take him shopping. That way he would be more satisfied to stay home.

Paw and I arrived at Mrs. Booksteen's house around 10 a.m. We were invited inside and into the living room. Paw rushed out through the French doors into the garden. I assumed he was looking for Arnold.

"Arnold has gone to Mr. Booksteen's shop to take his uncle his eyeglasses. I swear that man would forget his nose if it wasn't attached to his face." Mrs. Booksteen laughed. "I love him dearly but he can be exasperating."

I smiled at her and offered the cookies. "I baked these for the boys."

"Thank you, dear. I am sure they will enjoy them this afternoon. You know they are both really good boys. My sister has done a good job raising Arnold. Mr. Booksteen and I were never blessed with children, but if we had been, I would have wanted him to be like Arnold. And that poor boy, Billy. He is a good kid too. His stepdad is a rough man to get along with and a poor father if you ask me."

I must have looked alarmed for she rushed to add, "Oh, he doesn't beat the boy or anything. In fact, I think he loves him in his own way. It's just that he doesn't connect with the boy or try to understand him. So sad."

"I hope their relationship improves. It's nice that Billy can spend time with Arnold."

I walked toward the French doors. "I really can't stay, Mrs. Booksteen. Jac and I are going shopping this afternoon. She's on a quest to find the perfect gift for her dad's birthday. I have to get back home. I'll just collect Paw and we will be going."

We stepped outside into the garden. That is when I spied a large furry tail waving in the air as my dog dug furiously in Mrs. Booksteen's flower bed. I groaned. "Paw stop that at once!"

Hurrying over, I pulled on his collar. He went willingly because he had found his treasure. A dirty, lumpy, object coated in his drool.

"I am so sorry, Mrs. Booksteen. I will happily come over and repair the damage. I would be glad to buy you new flowers."

Mrs. Booksteen was staring thoughtfully at the object in my hand. "Yes, dear, we will work on the garden. Do you know what's in your hand?" For a minute, I thought Mrs. Booksteen was behaving oddly. Then I looked at what I was holding. Understanding began to dawn.

"Oh my, this is a teddy bear. Admittedly, a little rough for wear but still a bear. Do you think it is the one Billy lost?"

"I don't know. It would be awfully strange if it was some other bear." She frowned. "But how did it get buried in my flower bed? We looked thoroughly for it yesterday."

"I think I can answer that. My guess is that Paw took it while the boys played and buried it. He does love stuffed toys. I've seen him bury his own in the past. I never thought about him doing so yesterday. He could very well have buried it and planned to retrieve it for himself. At least it looks that way."

"Very possible. Well, let's take it inside and clean it up for Billy. Don't worry about the garden now. The boys can help me later today and if anything needs replacing we'll discuss it later."

We took the bear inside and planned how to clean it. Some stuffed animals do not bathe well so we decided to first brush as much dirt off it as we could. That is when we noticed a tear in the seam running down the bear's back. I was familiar with this kind of damage, as Paw does the same thing to his toys. Mrs. Booksteen volunteered some needle and thread so that I could sew it. Some of the stuffing appeared dirty so I began to pull it out as Mrs. Booksteen went upstairs to get some new stuffing. Being a crafter, Mrs. Booksteen had lots of supplies on hand.

I was pulling out stuffing when something clinked onto the floor. Looking down, I saw a small key. It was about an inch long and made of brass. Too small for a house key or safe deposit key.

Mrs. Booksteen had just returned and saw it too. "Now why would a key be in a stuffed bear?"

"I don't know. It is sure odd. I wonder if Billy knows about it."

Arnold returned home then, but he had no clue either. I shook my head. "What do you suppose we should do, Mrs. Booksteen? Should we replace it in the bear and sew it up or not?"

Mrs. Booksteen contemplated this for a minute. "Why not leave the bear with me? Arnold and I will ask Billy when he comes over later. I can sew the bear for him then and

A Dog Detective Short Story Collection

explain what happened. That key makes me nervous for some reason."

I agreed with her. "I have never seen a key like this. Have you?"

"No, but I may know who could identify it. Mr. Harper at the Hardware Store. He has to make lots of keys for people. He would be the most likely one to know about the key. Isn't that where you and Jac are going today?"

"Yes, it is. I don't want to take the key along. You need it to show Billy. I could draw a copy of it and take that, though."

"I have a better solution." She hurried off, returning with a Polaroid camera. She took a picture of the key and we waited for it to develop. Within a minute, I had a perfect photo of the key.

I thanked her and was about to leave with Paw when she said, "Why don't you leave Paw here with me and the boys? I am sure Arnold will keep him occupied and the boys would love his company."

Arnold implored, "Please can we keep him for a while."

"Well....If you are sure?" They both nodded. "Okay." I knelt down to Paw. He looked at me with his big, brown, soulful eyes. "You be on your best behavior," I told him. "No digging or mischief. And listen to Mrs. Booksteen and the boys." He gave me a big doggie smile and face lick. That meant he agreed.

I went home. Jac arrived shortly and we headed to the downtown shops. I told her everything that had happened at Mrs. Booksteen's house. She was intrigued and insisted we go to the Hardware Store first. That was its name - Hardware Store. Mr. Harper believed in the direct approach.

We stepped into the store. Mr. Harper was busy with a customer so I helped Jac choose a wrench for her dad. Jac and her dad adored and they doted on one another. I imagine this had a lot to do with the two of them only having each other. Jac's mother had passed away when she was very young and Jac had no other siblings. We soon found a wrench and went to the front of the store. By then, Mr. Harper had finished with the other customer.

"You ladies find what you were looking for?" He smiled at us.

"Yes. Thank you, Mr. Harper. I think this wrench is just what dad needs." Jac nodded as she sat the wrench on the counter.

"Good choice, Jac. Your dad is still working on the plumbing I assume."

"Definitely, and getting frustrated by the day. You know Dad - he won't give up, though."

"Mr. Harper," I asked, "I know you make lots of keys here. I have a photo of a key a friend and I found. I wondered if you had seen one like it or could identify it?"

Mr. Harper looked at the photo. "No problem. I have seen this kind of key lots of times. It goes to a toolbox."

"A toolbox?" Both Jac and I exclaimed.

"Yes. I sell the kind this key goes to. Here, let me show you." He walked back through the store as we followed. We stopped in front of a display of toolboxes and Mr. Harper

A Dog Detective Short Story Collection

lifted one down. It was 20 inches long by 8 inches wide and 8 inches deep. Black in color with the key attached by a string. The key was identical to the one I had found in the bear.

"You wouldn't happen to be able to tell me who in town owns such a toolbox, would you?" I asked hopefully.

Mr. Harper began shaking his head. "No. It is a popular item, besides I don't keep track of who buys what." His voice took on a tone of mild rebuke. "Even if I did, I wouldn't tell you because I value my customers' privacy."

"Fair enough, Mr. Harper. I'll just have to find another way to identify the owner." Jac was looking at the toolbox and decided to buy one for her dad.

"I wouldn't worry too much if I was you. Most people don't bother locking their toolboxes. They just like knowing they can if they need to." Mr. Harper rang up Jac's purchase and we left the store.

"So what now?" Jac asked as soon as we were out of the store.

"I'm not sure. I guess I'll go back and report to Mrs. Booksteen after we're done shopping. Maybe Billy will know something about the key."

"Do you really want to continue shopping? I got what I came for and I admit I am curious to find out the answer about the key too."

"I'm happy to skip shopping. Let's go back to Mrs. Booksteen's." We got in Jac's car and drove over there.

Mrs. Booksteen was surprised to see me again so soon. She was delighted that we had learned something about the key. Billy and Arnold were in the garden. Billy didn't know how the key got in his bear. He wasn't overly concerned about the bear either. His stepdad had bought it for him. He had told Mrs. Booksteen, "I ain't a baby. I don't need a bear." But she noted, he seemed happy for her to sew it up and clean it for him. She had left the key out.

We called the boys in for cookies and sat around discussing the garden. Jac showed them all the wrench she had bought for her dad. Arnold was interested since he liked tools. His dad did construction work and he wanted to build things someday, too. It was when Jac brought out the toolbox that Billy spoke.

"My stepdad has one of those."

"He does?" I said. "When did you see it?"

"A few weeks ago when Mrs. Booksteen was away on her trip. Dad buried it next to that new plant she wanted planted." He shrugged.

"My new rhododendron?" Mrs. Booksteen queried.

"Don't know what a rhododendron is, but I know he buried a box like that."

"Show us where, Billy," I urged.

We all trooped out of the house and he pointed to a spot next to Mrs. Booksteen's new rhododendron. "Right there."

"Shall we dig?" I asked her.

"Yes." Mrs. Booksteen answered.

"I'll get a shovel," I said, heading for her small shed.

Jac called me back. "No need. Paw is digging for it."

I hurried back, worried that Paw would dig up more than the box. Like the bush as well. I needn't have worried.

A Dog Detective Short Story Collection

He soon had the box uncovered. I pushed him out of the way and he shook himself vigorously spraying all of us with mulch and dirt. I lifted out the toolbox and we carried it into the house.

"Should we open it?" Jac asked.

Arnold cried, "Yes. Let's open it."

Billy pleaded, "Please."

"Technically, it is on Mrs. Booksteen's property so I believe it should be her decision." I looked to her for an answer.

"Open it," she said.

I inserted the key from Billy's bear into the lock and turned the key. With a click it opened. I unlatched the lid and lifted it. Inside were two books. The boys shook their heads as though to say who would want books. I removed the books. Underneath gleamed stacks of gold coins. The boys' eyes were as big as saucers. I imagine mine were too.

Mrs. Booksteen reached for the two books. She examined them carefully. "Interesting," she said.

Arnold asked, "What's so interesting about a book?"

Mrs. Booksteen shook her head. "Arnold, you need to learn to appreciate books more. Your Uncle Harold loves books. I can't get the man to stop reading. But these books are special. They are very old. I'm not an expert, but I think these are valuable. They look like first editions. Harold would know better."

"They are rare?" I asked.

"I think so."

"What do we do now?" Jac asked.

Pieces were starting to fall into place in my mind. I pondered what to do. "Mrs. Booksteen, when will Harold be home this evening? And Billy, where is your stepdad?"

Mrs. Booksteen said, "Harold would be home at 6 o'clock."

Billy shrugged. "He's at a meeting today. He told my mom that he would be home late."

I determined we needed to move quickly. To Mrs. Booksteen I said, "Could Harold stop home soon and look at those books? I have a question for him."

"I'll get him here within the hour," she replied and went to the phone.

I called Bruce after she was finished on the phone. This required a professional's assistance. He answered immediately and assured me he would be there in an hour. Both men arrived at the same time. Harold and Bruce discussed the books and agreed that they were rare and valuable.

I asked, "They came from the pawnshop robbery, didn't they?" Everyone looked bewildered but Bruce.

He nodded, saying, "I believe so. They fit with the titles and description from one of the robberies. We need to formulate a way to prove Mr. Reynolds' involvement and catch him and the rest of the criminals."

"I have a plan," I said. Bruce listened and agreed that it might work.

Harold went back to work with the promise to keep quiet about what we found. It was decided that the boys should remain with Mrs. Booksteen just in case Billy should slip and tell something to his mom or dad. We didn't believe his mom was involved, but we didn't want her in danger. Mrs. Booksteen opened a seam in the bear and replaced the key. Jac and I reburied the toolbox by the rhododendron. Then Mrs. Booksteen took the bear over to the Reynolds's house. She explained to Mrs. Reynolds that she found it in the hedge when she was clipping it. Mrs. Reynolds thanked her. She agreed that it would be fine for Mrs. Booksteen to keep Billy overnight to play with Arnold.

Bruce went into action setting the rest of the plan in motion. Jac hated to miss the possible action, but she needed to get home and make her dad supper. Paw and I stayed with Mrs. Booksteen and the boys. Later that evening, Harold returned home and Bruce joined us. Bruce set up surveillance on the garden.

It was midnight before Mr. Reynolds showed up. He crept through the hedge and turned to the row of rhododendrons. Bruce and I watched him from an upstairs bedroom. I had to hold Paw still and keep him quiet. Mr. Reynolds started digging where we had reburied the box. He began to lift the box from the dirt. That's when Bruce moved. Paw pulled from my grip and followed him. I rushed down the stairs behind them.

Outside, the moon shown down on two figures fighting. Mr. Reynolds hit Bruce in the leg with the toolbox. As Bruce stumbled, Paw leapt in the air and tackled Mr. Reynolds face first into the lawn. Paw kept Reynolds lying on the ground while emitting an occasional low growl.

Everyone else came running from the house. Bruce righted himself and walked over to Mr. Reynolds. Bruce tried to move

Paw, but he wasn't budging. Bruce looked at me and nodded toward Paw. I called Paw to come to me. He instantly jumped up and trotted to my side. Bruce handcuffed Mr. Reynolds and helped the man to his feet. He took Reynolds into the living room as the rest of us followed. Harold carried in the toolbox.

Reynolds refused to talk at first. Bruce found the key on him and opened the toolbox. Mrs. Booksteen had walked across and brought Mrs. Reynolds, Shelly, over to us. Mr. Reynolds still refused to speak.

"Harold," I said. "Didn't you deliver some books to Hawaii for Mr. Reynolds?"

"I did. He asked me to hand deliver them to a small surfing shop."

Bruce questioned, "Do you know the address?"

"I do." Harold affirmed.

"Good," Bruce said. "I am sure we can tie the books you delivered to those stolen in the pawnshop robberies. And these books," he picked up the two from the toolbox, "will surely tie in as well. Plus, these gold coins will make the case stronger." He turned to Mr. Reynolds. "Cooperate and you may receive a reduced sentence. Otherwise, you may be facing a long jail time."

Mrs. Reynolds asked him, "Is this true, Terrence? Did you commit these crimes?"

"It's not what you think. I didn't rob the pawnshops. It was Gary, my brother, and some of his friends. They are the ones stealing the stuff. I couldn't turn my own brother in to the police. He's family. Besides, we need the money. I

A Dog Detective Short Story Collection

figured it couldn't hurt to sell the stuff off. People didn't want it or they wouldn't have pawned it."

Mrs. Reynolds shook her head in disgust. "We don't need the money that bad. And don't you dare say it is for Billy's welfare. You never show him any kindness. I had hoped you would warm to him, but I was wrong. I want nothing more to do with you." She took Billy and left the house. Paw wanted to go, too, to comfort Billy, but I called him back. They needed time alone to adjust to everything that happened.

I couldn't help but ask, "But why bury the toolbox in Mrs. Booksteen's garden?"

"Some of Gary's friends weren't happy that Gary gave me some of the stuff to sell. I caught one of them snooping around the house. He saw me in the toolshed with the toolbox. I figured the safest place for the stuff was in Mrs. Booksteen's garden. No one would look for it there." Reynolds shrugged.

Bruce wanted to know, "Then why put the key in the bear?"

"No one is going to look for a key in a stuffed bear." Reynolds looked at Bruce as if he was stupid. "Like I said, Ken, one of my brother's friends, saw me that day in the shed locking the toolbox. I didn't trust him to search the house so I hid the box of stuff and the key so that no one could find it."

Mr. Booksteen exclaimed in shock, "Didn't you give a thought to what might happen to your wife or Billy if those guys did break in? Both your wife and son could have been in danger."

"Nah. Those guys knew Shelly and Billy didn't know anything. They wouldn't have bothered them."

Bruce shook his head at Reynolds's attitude. "The police will move quickly to arrest your brother, Gary, and his accomplices." He stood up, glancing around the room. "You'll all have to give statements, but I that can wait until morning."

In one hand, Bruce lifted the toolbox, with its incriminating evidence inside, and with the other hand he grasped Mr. Reynolds by the arm. "I'm taking you and the evidence to the police station tonight."

As Bruce left, he smiled at me. "I will let you know everything that happens in the morning."

Mrs. Booksteen hugged Arnold. "Go on up to bed."

He nodded and trudged up the stairs.

She turned to me. "I don't want you driving home this late. I want you and Paw to spend the night here."

I smiled. "Thank you, Mrs. Booksteen. We accept."

Soon I was climbing into bed. Paw leaped up and joined me. I ruffled his ears. "Billy may have his stuffed bear, but I have a real life furry best friend in you. Thank you for being the best dog detective I could ever dream of having."

He gave my face a long slurp, and curled up next to me. My world was just as it was meant to be.

5

THE MYSTERY OF THE MISSING ACTOR

1990s

"How is the play going?" I asked Shelbee. "It opens this Saturday, right?"

We were driving to the local forest to take a hike. It was early enough in the day that the summer sun wasn't too hot. Paudius Pernivious, nicknamed Paw, my very large Saint Bernard, was in the backseat.

"Not bad, from what I can tell. Everyone seems to know their lines. Robert is a big help. He has much more experience than everyone else but is very generous with his time and advice. Saturday night's opening should be a good performance. Are you and Bruce coming?" She slanted a sly glance my direction. Bruce Sever and I had formed a friendship a few months ago and ever since Shelbee and Jac believed we would make a perfect couple.

Shelbee Van Vight and Jac Weldon were my two best friends. We had gone to school together and formed a fast friendship when our teacher put us together for a spelling contest. The prize was ice cream cones and we were all determined to come in first. Our team won and we bonded over that ice cream. Friends ever since then.

"Clarissa Montgomery Hayes, are you going to answer my question or daydream?" Shelbee laughed. "What are you thinking about? Or, should I say whom?"

"All right, you caught me. I was daydreaming, or reminiscing, really. I was just thinking about the time we all met and won that ice cream."

"I remember that. They didn't have the flavor I wanted. No butter pecan. I had to settle for vanilla." Shelbee pretended to pout.

"A hardship, I know, since you love all kinds of ice cream," I teased her. "But to answer your question – Bruce and I will be at the play. He asked me to go with him a few days ago."

"Yes! Romance blooms," Shelbee cried.

"Okay, Ms. Romance; now tell me about Robert's pets. You said you have to feed them first, but you didn't mention it when we talked yesterday."

"That's because I didn't know. I had a note slipped under my front door with his key when I went home last night. Robert said he had to go out of town suddenly for the weekend. That's odd because he never said anything to the cast and he is the lead in the play. Ivan can handle it. He's

A Dog Detective Short Story Collection

Robert's understudy, but still, it will seem odd not having Robert there."

"Didn't you pet sit once before for him?"

"Yes. I pet sat for two days when he first came to town. That was a few months ago. He has a parrot and a cat. He asked me in person that time. I hope everything is all right. Which reminds me – we have to keep Paw outside. Robert's cat, Kathleen, doesn't like dogs, as I understand it."

"It's okay. I can keep Paw outside with me. We can walk around until you are done." My furry friend woofed from the backseat. Shelbee and I laughed at how he seemed to understand what we said.

Shelbee pulled into the driveway of a modest house in one of the town's subdivisions. Many of the houses were new, but some of the older houses were here as well. The builder had built homes around the older ones. Robert's house was one of the newer ones. A sign out front stated the house number and "Roberts."

"He missed the apostrophe in his name," I commented to Shelbee. My friends usually understand my odd remarks. I am a freelance writer and quick to see words that need editing. But this time Shelbee looked at me with confusion.

"What do you mean? It is spelled right. Robert's last name is Roberts." She smiled when she saw the look of doubt on my face. "I know Robert Roberts seems too convenient. Some of the other actors at the theater think it is a stage name. I don't know or care. He's been very decent to all of us."

"It just surprised me. I haven't met the man, but from

what you say, he has been very good to everyone at the theater and in town." I opened my car door and started to get out.

Shelbee was walking toward the front door. I planned to put Paw's leash on in the back seat and walk him in Robert's yard.

As I turned to close my door, Paw leaped over the backseat and jumped out. He raced toward the house then dodged to the left and raced around the side of the house.

I shouted, "Paw get back here!" I should have saved my breath. I knew he wouldn't listen when he was determined to go somewhere. I raced around the corner after him. Shelbee had followed me. I ran along the side of the house and turned right to the back. I had to stop suddenly so as not to run over Paw. Shelbee ran into the back of me.

"Why'd you stop?" I heard her grumble.

"Look." I pointed to Paw who stood half in the open back door. His shoulders were hunched and he was emitting a low growl. From inside the house could be heard a bird yelling at the top of his voice, "No! John! No!" repeatedly.

"Pedro!" Shelbee pushed past Paw through the door before I could caution her to wait.

Paw took this as permission to enter too.

I followed more cautiously.

I stepped into a kitchen that was a mess. Literally. In front of me, there was a center island where food lay scattered across the top. A bottle of wine was tipped over spilling its contents across the island and dripping to the floor. What appeared to be a wine glass lay shattered on the floor. I grabbed Paw's collar to keep him from the glass, but he pulled from my grasp and ran through the door to the next room.

Stepping around the food, I made my way to the door. The next room appeared to be a living room. A chair was overturned and a briefcase lay on the floor scattering papers everywhere. Several books from a bookcase were on the floor as well. The parrot, Pedro, was frantically pacing the perch in his cage, setting it to swing on the hook to which it was attached.

Shelbee was cooing to the bird, trying to calm him down.

He kept repeating, "No! John! No!" Then he screamed "Kathleen!"

Shelbee cried, "Oh my God, I forgot about her. We have to find Kathleen."

She knelt and looked under the sofa.

"Shelbee, we need to call the police. Something criminal happened here."

"You go call. I'm going upstairs to find her." Shelbee stood up and started toward the front of the house where I assumed the stairs were.

"Shelbee, it's not safe. Suppose the intruder is still here!"

Shelbee wouldn't listen.

"No. Kathleen is my responsibility. I have to find her. You'd do the same if it were Paw."

Paw woofed in agreement. He had been staring mesmerized by the bird, but now he ran to follow Shelbee.

"All right, we'll look around, but let me call the police first."

Shelbee nodded.

I went to the small desk in the corner where Robert's phone sat. I pulled down my sleeves to hold the receiver and punch buttons. I didn't want to compromise the crime scene any more than we already had. The dispatcher said she was sending a police officer immediately and told me to go back outside. *We would*, I thought, as soon as we looked for Kathleen.

I turned to the front of the house to follow Shelbee. As I moved, I noticed one of the books on the floor had a drop of blood on it. It was the only blood I had seen. Bending down, I took a closer look. I didn't dare pick it up for fear of contaminating any evidence. The blood looked dried. How old it was I didn't know. The book appeared to be a language translation book: English to French. I noticed several of the other books were on languages as well – German, Russian, and Spanish. Shelbee had told me that Robert was considered a consummate actor. I guess he used languages as part of his roles.

I went upstairs to a short hallway with three doors off it. The first door I pushed open revealed a bathroom. There was no closet, and I could see under or behind everything in the room. No cat.

The second door was partially open, and when I went in, I found Shelbee and Paw on either side of the bed. Each one had their head stuck under it. It would have been an amusing sight if not for the seriousness of the situation.

A Dog Detective Short Story Collection

"She's not here." Shelbee looked bereft. "I've checked all the rooms. No sign of her. She must have run out the open back door. What am I going to do? How will I explain this to Robert?"

"I'm beginning to think something happened to Robert, Shelbee." She looked at me with concern. I continued, "This doesn't look like a robbery. Someone had a struggle downstairs. His briefcase is down there, too. I remember you telling me that everyone joked with him at the theater about the fact that he went everywhere with it. So why didn't he take it with him?"

"You're right. I was too concerned for Pedro to pay attention to it. Let's go down and I will look at it."

We all went downstairs where Shelbee confirmed that it looked to be his briefcase. She bent down to look at the papers on the floor. "This is the script for the play. See where Robert made notations in the margin? He always scribbled."

"Shelbee." She looked up at me. "Is that the same writing as on Robert's note?"

"No." She sighed. "The note I received was typed. I never thought about it." We both looked around Robert's living room, but could see no typewriter.

In the distance, I heard a police siren. "Come on, let's get out of here. The dispatcher wanted us outside. I think it best we look like we complied when the officer gets here."

We trooped outside to the front and had about thirty seconds before the police car pulled up.

I recognized the officer who stepped out of the cruiser.

His name was Steven Heldman. I know most everyone on the police force because my uncle is the chief of police. Uncle Harry was out of town for a conference, or I am sure he would have been on the scene since the dispatcher knew my voice.

"Ma'am. Ms. Hayes." The officer nodded to us. "Please tell me what the problem is."

We explained why we were there and what we had seen. The officer informed us to stay outside while he went to look around.

"This is going to scare Kathleen worse if she is hanging around," Shelbee groaned. "I should be checking the bushes around the house and at the neighbors."

"While he's inside, let's look out front here." I figured we had a few minutes. Of course, that didn't turn out to be true.

"What are you ladies doing?" The officer's voice made us both jump. He was a silent walker. We had been peeking under the few bushes around the front door.

Shelbee crossed her arms. "Looking for Mr. Roberts's cat. I'm his pet sitter and I'm worried she got out."

The officer stood firm. "This is a crime scene, ladies. You need to stay back away from the house."

Paw looked like he was about to growl at the man so I hunched down and patted his head.

The officer gave Paw a cautious look. "Now, please go stand on the sidewalk."

I grasped Shelbee's arm and Paw's leash, pulling them to the sidewalk.

A Dog Detective Short Story Collection

The officer detached his radio from his shoulder. "I need backup at …"

A silver sedan pulled up next to us. To my surprise, it was Bruce. He got out, came around the car, and gave Paw a pet and hugged me. Over his shoulder, Shelbee smirked at me. He nodded to her.

"Are you two all right?"

"We're fine," I said. "How did you know we were here?"

"I have a police radio in the car. Your name was mentioned when the call came through." He smiled as I groaned. Harry was sure to hear about this and give me a lecture about staying out of police business.

The officer returned, and to my surprise, welcomed Bruce. "Mr. Sever. I guess you heard the call."

Bruce nodded.

"I have more officers on the way. I need to get these ladies' statements and then you can leave."

Shelbee asked, "But what about Pedro and Kathleen?"

The officer looked stunned. "Who are they?"

"Mr. Roberts's pets. Pedro is in the house. He's the parrot and he's very upset." I could see the officer's eyes light up when she mentioned Pedro. If you weren't used to a parrot, they could be quite noisy. "You already know about Kathleen. She is the cat we were looking for. Pedro needs to be fed and Kathleen needs to be found. They are my responsibility."

The officer looked about ready to protest, but Bruce intervened. "Officer Heldman, I can vouch for both ladies.

Why not let Shelbee take Pedro to the local vet? He will be safe there."

Shelbee turned to Bruce. "But what about Kathleen? She will be scared by all the police." As she said this, two more cruisers pulled up to the curb.

"Shelbee, I understand, but we can't get in the way of the investigation. We have to stay away from the house. I'm sure the officers will look for her." Turning, he spoke to Officer Heldman. "Would you let her look around the neighborhood? Surely, that wouldn't do any harm. I can go in with you, get Pedro, and take him to the vet."

"That will be okay as long as she doesn't get near the crime scene. Also, she needs to give her statement before she leaves." Shelbee readily agreed and gave her statement. I went next while Bruce went inside to get Pedro.

He came out and let Shelbee talk to Pedro a few minutes. Paw was by her side the whole time. The parrot fascinated him.

Leaning over to Bruce, I whispered, "Thank you."

He smiled at me. "Just be careful. I don't like the way that house looks. I doubt the criminal is still around, but I want you to avoid anyone or any place that looks suspicious."

I nodded. Shelbee loaded Pedro in Bruce's car and he drove away.

Shelbee and I decided to walk up the sidewalk and then circle around behind the houses. A field lay in back that would make a good hiding place for Kathleen. Several people were outside on their front lawns, no doubt drawn there by the police sirens. We were stopped by several of

Robert's neighbors who wanted to know what was happening. We gave a brief, carefully-edited, version of events. We asked everyone we saw if they had seen Kathleen. No one knew anything nor had they seen the cat.

We were both discouraged, but decided to go back to the field and call Kathleen's name. Paw was enjoying himself immensely. Nearly everyone had adored him and wanted to pet him. He was happy to go over to the field, too. Lots of interesting scents and sights out there.

Just as we stepped into the field, a rabbit ran out from its cover and raced ahead of us. Paw lunged to run after it. Paw is hefty and strong so it was all I could do to hold onto him. Being that I am small at just a few inches over five feet, Paw is as big as me. I do yoga and go walking and hiking, but Paw challenges all my muscles pulling on the leash. Fortunately, Shelbee reached over and grabbed hold of his collar.

"Weightlifting," she said to me with a meaningful stare. She had been trying to get me to lift weights for months. I confess I would rather lift a good book, especially a mystery.

I grunted in reply. Paw had settled down and was sitting with his tongue lolling out the side of his mouth.

Shelbee pointed to a small red car parked behind a house. "There is Robert's car." I realized that we were standing directly behind Robert's house. Fortunately, we were in the field, a good distance from the house since I could see the officer who we had spoken to standing at Robert's kitchen door.

"I hadn't noticed it when we were at the house. I was distracted by the mess in the kitchen."

Shelbee frowned. "He should have taken his car. Now I'm even more worried."

We decided to keep walking through the field calling Kathleen's name. So far, no response or sight of her. By now, it was close to lunch, and we had walked a good distance from Robert's house.

My stomach rumbled. "I'm starving. I think we need to stop for a while and get some lunch." I nodded at Paw. "He needs some water. It's getting hot out here."

Shelbee sighed but nodded assent. "I hate leaving her like this. She's got to be scared."

"I know. But she's more likely to come back when it's quieter." A lawn mower started as I said this. The neighborhood was getting busy with people out doing their lawn chores.

Shelbee nodded again and we turned to the houses.

We angled ourselves to reach Roberts's road about a block away from his house. Our car was still parked out front and we wanted to reach it without disturbing the police any more than we had to. We were a few houses away when we came alongside a classic white house with a white picket fence. Paw jumped up, placed his paws on the fence and woofed.

An elderly gentleman stood up on the other side of the fence. "Hey, there, big fella. How are you?" He laughed looking at Paw.

The gentleman smiled at me. "All right to pet him?"

I nodded.

He gave Paw a good scratch behind the ears.

"I hope he didn't scare you," I said by way of apology. "We didn't know you were there."

"No problem. Believe it or not, I love dogs. Thirty-five years with the post office and never bit. Just got to know how to communicate with them. This fella looks like he is a real intelligent one."

I smiled and pointed to Paw. "His name is Paw. This is my friend Shelbee, and I'm Clarissa. We are looking for a gray and black, long-haired cat. Have you seen her?"

"No. Sorry. Can't say that I saw a cat. Now if you had asked me about a rusted brown van going down the alley last night, I could help you." He pointed at the narrow alley which ran between his house and the next one.

Shelbee suddenly straightened. "A rusted brown van? Anything else you could tell me about it?"

He shrugged. "Looked to me like a faded eagle decal on the side. 'Course my eyes aren't as good as they used to be. You're the second person to ask about it. One of them young deputies asked me just a few minutes ago. Do you think it's important?"

Shelbee was lost in thought so I answered. "Could be. You never know. Thanks for telling us. If you see a cat, please let me know." I handed him one of my business cards. I rarely had a reason to hand one out.

"A writer, eh? Maybe you can put a character like me in one of your books someday?" He winked at me.

I smiled. "Maybe." I didn't have the heart to tell him that

I mostly wrote for magazines. I was having a hard time getting the book I was working on completed.

We said goodbye to him, Paw gave a final woof, and we walked to our car. I gave Paw some fresh water in a bowl I carried with me. Shelbee was still distracted. Once in the car, I turned to her and asked, "What's the matter?"

"That van he mentioned? We use one like it at the theater. It belongs to one of the actors. What are the odds there are two rusted brown vans with a faded eagle on it in town?"

"I wouldn't bet on it." Paw woofed in agreement. "Let's have a late lunch and then go to the theater to ask around. They're rehearsing this afternoon, right?"

"Yes. They are doing a final run through for opening night. According to rumor, some talent agent is supposed to be there for the opening performance. They want to have their performances perfect in case he decides to represent them." Shelbee pointed to a picnic area under some trees. "Why don't we stop here to eat? I packed plenty of food this morning when I thought we would be hiking."

"Sounds good to me."

Paw eagerly followed the picnic basket to one of the picnic tables. We enjoyed a leisurely lunch. Paw got some of my sandwich along with some dog food. His vet kept cautioning me not to feed him junk food, but I must admit I was a pushover. Healthy fresh veggies and meat were fine, as part of a vet approved diet that provided the right calories and nutrients, but Paw loved junk food. His adorable begging expression, with big brown eyes, caused me to relent more times than I wanted to admit.

We drove to the theater after lunch and parked in the side lot. Shelbee directed us to walk around the back first. We found the van parked there. It was distinctive with the faded eagle decal. I couldn't see how there could be two alike.

Shelbee opened the back doors. "The van is used to transport props plus conduct other theater business. It's available for use by anyone at the theater, and the keys are usually kept under the visor on the driver's side. So anyone could have used it."

I looked through the doors. "I'm still not sure the van had anything to do with Roberts's disappearance."

Of course, Paw had to jump up into the van and investigate. He managed to find a leftover sandwich on the floor. I scrambled into the van to take it from him. Who knew how long it had lain there? I may give him people food, but I didn't trust something that lay in the back of a van.

My knee came down on a sharp object. "Ouch!"

I grabbed onto Paw's collar and lifted my knee. Under it lay a small oddly-shaped metal object with a tack sticking up. I brushed it to the end of the van's bed and Paw and I got out of the van.

Shelbee came over to examine the object.

Paw looked forlornly at the sandwich he knew he wasn't going to get to eat.

"This is Robert's tie tack. I would recognize it anywhere.

It is a flag. See." She pointed to horizontal stripes of white, blue, and red. "He said a special friend gave it to him."

"Could he have lost it while using the van? Just because his tie tack is here doesn't mean the van was connected to his disappearance. It could be someone else's, too."

"I doubt it. I'm sure he had it on at yesterday's rehearsal. He considers it good luck and says he always wears it right before a performance. Besides, he left in his car before me yesterday."

"Does anyone else wear this tie tack?"

"No. I don't think any of the others ever wear a tie, let alone a tie tack. We're all mostly jeans and t-shirt type of people." Shelbee's brow scrunched. "Let's go inside. Maybe some of the others will know something."

We entered the theater through the back door. Voices could be heard on the stage. Various individuals were hurrying back and forth doing who knows what. I had very little experience with theaters, but Shelbee seemed to think everything was normal.

The voices on stage became more distinct.

"George, move more stage right."

"Sarah, you need to limp more. You're an old woman. Practice with that cane."

"John, when you hit Ivan, make the swing bigger. Really exaggerate it. The audience in the back can't see as well."

"Ivan, try to project more. You know how Robert did it. Follow his example."

Sarah asked, "Where is he anyway? We need him here."

Ivan huffed. "Why? I can do this role."

The director's voice cut in. "Of course, you can. We're just all worried about him. Everybody take a few minutes to relax and we'll come back refreshed."

Shelbee smiled at me. "That's Jon Kenyon. He's the director. When Robert's here, Jon often consults with him on the direction, but he's a great director on his own."

We walked over and she introduced me. Mr. Kenyon appeared to be in his thirties with a short cropped haircut and piercing blue eyes.

Jon shook my hand. He looked down at Paw and sneezed. Paw backed up and looked at him questioningly.

He waved us away. "Sorry. Allergies. Never could have a pet since I was young. Please take him outside."

I nodded, murmuring apologies, and hurried Paw outside. Shelbee stayed behind to talk to Jon.

Outside a few of the actors were chatting. They looked up when I came out. Paw growled at the group. Shocked, I stammered apologies and pulled him a distance away.

"What is it, buddy?" I hunkered down next to him and pet his head. I was surprised at his behavior. Normally, he liked most people. Paw seemed to calm down as I pet him.

The group had resumed talking.

The woman named Sarah said, "I still think John needs a stage name."

John huffed. "Why? If you ask me, this changing names is a waste of time. It won't make a difference to that talent scout."

George laughed. "What's the harm? Besides, Ivan's using

your name for his stage name. You might as well pick one for yourself."

John grunted. "I won't be using Ivan; that's for sure."

Ivan protested, "What's wrong with my name?"

John growled, "If you like it so much, why do you want to change it?"

Ivan glowered.

Paw tensed at the anger in John's voice.

I tugged on his collar, walking him further away from the group.

As I moved away, I heard Sarah speak calmly. "John, Ivan, we're just playing around with new names. You know this started when we all thought Robert used a stage name."

The rest of their conversation faded away.

George, John, Ivan, and Sarah turned when the back door opened and Shelbee came out. They greeted her as she joined them. She must have told them about Robert because there were exclamations of surprise from them. I couldn't hear what they said but guessed they were questioning Shelbee. Soon the group broke up, and Shelbee and Sarah walked over to me. Paw seemed content to see both of them.

"Sarah. This is my friend, Clarissa. And this is Paw." She gestured to him with a flourish.

She spoke with gusto. "Hello. And hello big boy. All right to pet him?"

I nodded yes and watched carefully, prepared to pull Paw back if need be. I needn't have worried. With a happy woof and big grin, he lapped up Sarah's attention.

A Dog Detective Short Story Collection

"Sarah is a pet sitter, too," Shelbee explained.

Sarah stroked Paw's ears. Paw turned his head and snuffled at the bandage on her hand. "Poor Kathleen. I hope you find her soon. And poor Robert. I shiver to think what happened to him."

"What happened?" I nodded at her bandage.

She laughed. "Cat scratch. One of my clients didn't want to take her medicine. Goes with the job. I'm sure Shelbee has the same war wounds."

Shelbee laughed, too. "It is inevitable."

Something niggled at the back of my brain, but I couldn't catch it.

Sarah laughed again. "We're going to be the bandage crew for this show. Jon, our director, and John Moore, he plays Frederick, both have bandages. And Ivan's been wearing a cloth brace for his carpal tunnel. We'll have to do something with wardrobe for opening night." She went on talking to Shelbee about wardrobe changes, but I wasn't listening.

A sudden idea had caught in my brain. There had been specks of blood on one of Roberts's books. Could Kathleen have caused it by scratching the intruder? If so, could one of the theater people have been the one scratched? I looked over at Sarah. She seemed nice enough and Paw liked her. It didn't mean she wasn't involved, but I trusted Paw's judgment. But he had backed away from Jon and growled at the chatting group. Could George, Jon, Ivan, or John Moore be involved?

Suddenly, I remembered Pedro's words, *No John No.*

Jon or John Moore - could it be one of them Pedro was identifying?

I needed to know more about where they had been last night.

Just then, Shelbee came up to me. Sarah had gone back into the theater as I was thinking.

"I know that look. You've figured something out."

"I'm not sure," I explained my theories to her.

Shaking her head, she said, "I can't see it of Jon Kenyon, our director. He is a great guy. As for John Moore, I don't know him that well."

"What we need to do is determine where they were last night," I mused. "And if either one of them had the van."

A voice behind us said, "What are you two up to?" We both jumped having been so absorbed in thought. Paw stood wagging his tail. Turning, I saw Bruce had joined us.

Shelbee asked eagerly, "How's Pedro?"

"He is loving life. The vet techs are pampering him and he is quoting Shakespeare. It took him a while to settle down, but he is fine now."

Shelbee sighed with relief.

I greeted him with a smile. "To answer your question: we think we have an idea who might have been involved in Robert's disappearance. Have the police determined anything yet?"

He smiled back. "They know about the van. I assume that is why you are here. They should be here soon."

"Yes. We found a tie tack of Robert's in the van. But no sign of him. I hope he is all right somewhere. I guess we

A Dog Detective Short Story Collection

messed up another crime scene by picking up the tack." I sighed ruefully.

"Let me see the tack." I handed it to him. "Probably too small to fingerprint, but I'll take it and explain to the police. What are you two planning next?"

I was glad to see he was supporting us. "We need to find out where Jon and John were last night."

George Rill, one of the actor's stepped out the back door. Shelbee waved him over. "Hey, George, got a minute?" He nodded and ambled over. Paw greeted him with a happy wave of his tail.

Shelbee continued, "Any idea what time everybody left last night after rehearsal?"

"Well, Sarah left shortly after you. She had to tend Miss Mac's cat. Then Johnny Moore left. He said he had an appointment, but didn't say where. Ivan left, too. That surprised me because he's been angling for the lead role and since Robert left before you, I assumed he would try to convince Jon to let him do one night in the lead. Guess something came up. That was around 7 pm, I guess. Jon and I stayed to discuss the props. We were having difficulties with one of the prop guns. Then I left about 8 pm. I assume Jon left shortly after. Why do you ask?"

Shelbee looked at me. I trusted Paw's judgment and he seemed to like George. I decided to explain our concerns and that the police would probably be there asking questions soon.

"That so?"

"Any idea where John Moore went? Or if Jon took

the van?"

"Don't know if Jon took the van, but I doubt it. He usually walks to the theater. Says he hates driving. Beats me; I'd rather drive than walk." He looked over his shoulder. "Now you didn't hear this from me, okay? I'm pretty sure John M goes out to the tavern on the highway every night after rehearsals. I think he's got a drinking problem."

A police cruiser pulled in.

Bruce cautioned George. "Keep our suspicions to yourself."

Bruce went to talk to the officers. They took our statements and the tie tack and politely told us to leave.

By now, it was getting late in the afternoon. Shelbee wanted to return to Robert's neighborhood to look for Kathleen. Bruce suggested that he could go to the tavern and check on Moore's alibi. Meanwhile, Paw and I could help Shelbee look for Kathleen. Tomorrow we could check up on Jon's whereabouts the night Robert went missing.

Shelbee, Paw, and I got into her car and headed to Robert's house. We parked in his driveway and walked around back. The neighborhood seemed quiet for a Saturday evening. We both started calling for Kathleen. There was no sign of her around the house. Shelbee had brought a can of cat treats and kept shaking them. This had Paw following her everywhere.

We decided to walk through the field again and go further down the neighborhood. Some of the homes at the end of the development were older and unoccupied. Perhaps Kathleen had hidden in one of them.

A Dog Detective Short Story Collection

I kept a tight grasp on Paw's leash. Several birds flew up out of the field, but my real concern was more rabbits. Paw loved to chase them. We were getting close to the older homes when we heard a rustling in a nearby bush. Paw instantly went alert. We watched as a furry head poked out. It looked at us and then stepped out toward us.

Shelbee cried, "Kathleen!"

The cat was a mix of gray and black with long hair and tufts on her ears. Bits of grass stuck to her fur. Her tail was erect indicating she was happy to see us. She meowed plaintively to us.

I was so startled when Paw lunged at her I lost my grip on his leash. He immediately ran at Kathleen. She turned and ran back to the houses with Paw in hot pursuit.

I ran after Paw with Shelbee close behind me. We were both yelling for Paw to stop. Shelbee soon passed me since she had much longer legs. I was huffing and puffing as I exited the field and came out behind the older homes. I was just in time to see Kathleen slip through a cat door in one of the older homes. Paw ran full out into the door. He bounced off and shook himself. Shelbee was soon there on her hands and knees talking to Kathleen through the door. She had to keep pushing Paw out of the way.

I approached more slowly to catch my breath. As I did, I noticed the house appeared to be unoccupied. There were no curtains at the windows or lights on in the house. No outdoor furniture and the grass looked like it needed to be mowed. The cat door was set in what appeared to be a small door to the garage.

"She isn't coming out," Shelbee said to me as I got to the door. We could hear her meowing plaintively. It sounded as if she was scolding us. Paw kept jumping up at the door to look in, but someone had covered the window in the door with black plastic.

I grabbed Paw's collar and hauled him back from the door. I said to Shelbee, "Try shaking the can. Maybe with Paw back, she will come out."

Shelbee tried this and Kathleen stepped cautiously out. Paw was surprisingly quiet. But when Shelbee reached to pick her up, Kathleen slipped back inside. Paw started barking as well.

"I get the feeling they want us to go inside," Shelbee said, looking up at me. I nodded in agreement.

Shelbee tried the door, but it was locked.

Paw had stopped barking, and it was then that I could hear a muffled cry.

Shelbee heard it too.

It didn't sound like a cat.

"I think we will have to break in. Here, hold Paw, and I will try something. This lock looks pretty simple. Maybe I can slide a credit card in the lock and get it to open."

Shelbee smirked at me. "Did Bruce teach you that?"

"Yes, he did. And no smirking."

It took several attempts by which time the muffled noises were growing more frequent.

Finally, the door opened.

We rushed inside to find Kathleen sitting on a man tied to a chair.

"Robert!" Shelbee hurried to him. He was gagged and his hands and feet were tied to the arms and legs of a chair. The garage was surprisingly full of stuff and boxes. I had thought the house seemed deserted.

Shelbee untied Robert's gag while I searched for something to cut the ropes that tied him to the chair.

Robert sighed in relief as the gag was removed. "Thank you, Shelbee. That's much better. I can't tell you how glad I am to see you. My kotyonok has been trying to keep me company. But I feared I would never be found."

"Kotyonok?" I asked.

"It means kitten. It is Russian. The land of my birth," Robert replied. By now, I had found a pair of clippers and was trying to cut through the ropes."

"Oh," I said.

Then, "Oh."

I realized I had made an error in my theories. Too late, I heard Paw growl and Kathleen hiss. I looked to the door to find Ivan standing there with a gun pointed at us.

"You?" Shelbee said with shock. "But I thought it was one of the Johns. Especially after Pedro was yelling, *No. John. No.*"

Ivan scowled at her but huffed, "Neither of them could be smart enough to pull this off. They both were in *his* shadow." He pointed the gun at Robert. "He's not the only one who can act, you know. He was going to hog all the attention, and that talent scout would have discovered him. But with Robert out of the way, I would have the lead role and get the deal."

I said, "You took the van to kidnap Robert."

"Of course. I wasn't going to use my car. The van is so convenient. It was easy to knock him out. I am much stronger. He may be Russian, but he doesn't have a Russian's strength. I wouldn't have had much of a struggle if it hadn't been for that cat jumping at me. That bird squawked so much I could not think. But I succeeded in the end."

"You don't have carpal tunnel, I assume." I was trying to keep him talking. There was a shovel to my left about a foot away, but I didn't know how I would reach it and get to him before he had a chance to fire. Shelbee was further away and Robert was still tied up.

Paw had laid down and was inching towards Ivan.

"Of course not. That blasted cat scratched me. I had to cover it somehow and the wrist brace was a convenient excuse."

"That's why there was blood at the scene," I said, trying to distract Ivan from Paw's creeping closer to him.

Ivan inclined his head to me. "You may be smarter than I thought. Now. You will all step back behind Robert. Sadly, it has become necessary for me to kill you two along with Robert. The dog and cat will have to die as well."

Shelbee hollered, "No," just as Paw lunged for Ivan's gun arm.

Kathleen launched herself from Robert's lap and landed on Ivan's head. The gun dropped from Ivan's hand as Paw bit deeper. I grabbed the shovel as Shelbee grabbed a baseball bat.

Robert shouted, "Kathleen!"

A Dog Detective Short Story Collection

The cat immediately dropped from Ivan's head.

I hit Ivan with the shovel.

He crumpled to the floor.

Paw stood guard over him.

I kicked the gun out of Ivan's reach and checked his pulse. He was still alive but would have a terrible headache. We untied Robert and tied up Ivan. He remained unconscious.

Shelbee ran down the street to the nearest house to call the police. She was back within ten minutes to report the police were on their way.

Shelbee looked at me. "There is still one thing I don't understand." I nodded for her to go ahead. "Pedro yelled the word, *John*. But it was Ivan who was the culprit."

Robert said, "I can answer that." We turned to him. "Everyone at the theater believed Robert Roberts was a stage name. The actors wanted to have stage names, too. Ivan chose to call himself John.

"He came to my house to rehearse on several occasions and insisted he be called John. Pedro will pick up on what I say, of course, and I can only image that in the struggle, I yelled John instead of Ivan."

The police and paramedics soon arrived along with Bruce who grabbed me in a big hug. "Are you all right? Paw?" He scanned me from head to toe for injuries. I nodded, pleased that he had included Paw in his concern.

Shelbee came up to us. "I'm fine too." She smiled to show she was not offended that Bruce hadn't asked about her.

The police took our statements and told us to go home.

The paramedics placed Robert on a stretcher. "We're taking Mr. Roberts to the hospital. He's dehydrated, and the lump on his head needs attention. He'll probably be required to stay the night."

The officer nodded. "I've taken his statement." He waved them away.

Robert held up a hand. "Shelbee, can you please take care of Kathleen?"

Shelbee hugged Kathleen, who purred contentedly. "Of course, I'll take her to the vet to check her health."

Robert reached over and caressed Kathleen's fur. "Be a good girl, kotyonok."

She meowed and purred louder.

The five of us – Bruce, Shelbee, Paw, Kathleen, and I – rode in Bruce's car down the street to where Shelbee had parked her car when we first went searching for Kathleen. It seemed like days ago but had only been a few hours. Paw and Kathleen had become fast friends. Neither complained about riding with the other.

Paw and I opted to ride home with Bruce and waved a farewell and a woof to Shelbee.

Bruce turned to me. "I was so worried when I heard the call on the police radio. Promise me you will be more careful from now on."

I smiled reassuringly. "I promise to be more careful. Believe me, I don't want to repeat this experience."

It seemed only minutes before we were parked in front of my house. The evening was cooling from the heat of the day.

The blooms of my daylilies, edging the paved walk to my porch, brightened my brick house.

Bruce walked around the car, opened my door, took my hand, and escorted me onto my porch. His hands were warm and strong.

He smiled at me. "I am so glad you are all right," he said, for perhaps the tenth time that evening.

I squeezed his hands, taking comfort to have him with me.

Paw sat at my heels, tail swishing gently across the porch boards, quietly breathing as if he was waiting for something to happen.

Bruce leaned forward. He pressed a tender kiss to my lips.

He stepped back, his deep brown eyes twinkling. "I'll see you tomorrow evening. I'm sure Robert will be spectacular in the play."

"Yes," I nodded, breathless from his kiss. "I'm sure you're right." I squeezed his hands. "Thank you for all your help."

He held my gaze. "I will always be there for you, Clarissa. Never doubt it."

He kissed my hand, then turned, and walked to his car.

He gave a final wave then drove away.

I knelt down to Paw. "I know. You are always there for me, too. Thank you for saving my life again."

He put his paw on my knee and woofed.

"I love you, too, Paw." I hugged him. "I love you, too."

REVIEW REQUEST

THANK you for reading. I truly appreciate your taking time from your busy day to read my novel. I know your time is limited, but could you do me a favor? Could you leave a review of this story? Reviews are an important part of a writer's marketing success.

Please see the *About the Author* page to contact Ms. Baublitz, and don't forget to sign up for the newsletter on her site to be the first to get updates on upcoming publications!

ABOUT THE AUTHOR

Sandra Baublitz is a lover of all animals. She has always loved dogs and cats. A Dog Detective series originally began as a contest entry. Paw's creation was influenced by the Beethoven movies and the author's desire to own a Saint Bernard. The author never got the opportunity to own a St. Bernard and her current cats will not allow a new edition. Ms. Baublitz expresses her love of the breed by continuing to write about Clarissa and Paw and their mystery adventures. She hopes her readers enjoy reading them as much as she enjoys writing them.

Please don't forget to sign up for the newsletter on her site to be the first to get updates on upcoming publications!

sandrabaublitz.com

OTHER BOOKS BY SANDRA BAUBLITZ

Short Stories:

The Mystery of the Blue Dolphins
The Mystery of Aunt Carol's Disappearance
The Mystery of the Body in the Shed
The Mystery of the Missing Bear
The Mystery of the Missing Actor

Novels:

Mastiffs, Mystery, and Murder
Bassets and Blackmail

Printed in Great Britain
by Amazon